SUNRIVER
LITE

A COLLECTION
compiled by
THE WRITERS GROUP
of
The Sunriver Arts Association

Sunriver Lite

ISBN-0-9634757-1-1

Address all inquiries to the Sunriver Writers Group
P.O. Box 3082, Sunriver, OR 97707

Printed by Maverick Publications, Inc.
Bend, Oregon

TABLE OF CONTENTS

CARTOONS

INSPIRATION

We're Writing About A Special Place

The Writers Group of Sunriver offers this collection of essays, short stories, and poems about life in Sunriver. We hope you enjoy them and they add to your understanding and enjoyment of this unique, wonderful community.

You'll find this is not a collection of the normal statistical information of Sunriver and its residents. You undoubtedly already know that Sunriver is a first cousin to the Garden of Eden, that it is located out in the middle of nowhere near Bend, Oregon, that it has a normal population of about 1,500 souls, but because it is a resort community, it is never normal and may swell to 10,000 to 12,000 on a busy weekend.

You may also know by now the main things which make people buy a house or condo in Sunriver. They are drawn here by the magnificent natural beauty, serenity, and isolation of the place. They see a way to play all of the golf and do all the skiing they want, ride bikes or jog till they are dizzy, or fish for trout in dozens of beautiful spots of splendid isolation. Or all of the above.

Almost all of us arrived here as curious tourists. We might have been part of a college fraternity party, a church retreat group, a business conference, a participant in a ski or golf package tour, attending a family reunion or wedding. We might have just heard about Sunriver from someone and, being adventurous, decided to go poking about on our own.

Regardless of how we got here, here we are. Some of us are young families, some of us are retired couples. Some of us are here by ourselves, trying to get a job or write a book or

1

paint or conduct business on the Internet. Some of us live here part time, most of us travel a lot. Virtually none of us are here unless we want to be.

Why is that? What is the magic? After all, one would think that we'd get sick of looking at the view, of fighting the long, cold winters, of driving miles to get the mail, of buying our clothes out of catalogues, of putting up with noisy tourists in the rental house next door.

How can a few thousand souls be so enthusiastic about living out in the piney forest, miles from anywhere, shoveling snow, scared to death of forest fires, skidding on ice-covered highways to go to the drug store? No amount of statistics can answer this question. We need to deal in psychology and culture and life-styles to begin to comprehend.

This is not a job for one writer. A lot of us need to tell our stories, to furnish testimonials about this great place. No one views life here quite the same as the next person. The essays and stories and poems which follow are written by a whole bunch of folks. Each tries to tell a small vignette of some aspect of living in Sunriver, all bound by our love and enthusiasm.

When you've finished reading all of them, we hope that you will have enjoyed yourselves and will understand why we're happy campers in a very special place.

IF HEAVEN ISN'T LIKE THIS, I'M COMING BACK

By
Norma Hodge

Sunriver is a very special place. Everyone says so: residents, non-residents and visitors. They're right. It IS special. The clean brisk air, the beautiful river and mountains, the altitude. But it's more than that.

What some visitors don't know and many residents do – is the spirit of the people who live here. Sunriver Spirit. It adopts a pathway and keeps it litter-and weed-free. It stops to help someone when they're injured or confused on the pathway. It encourages neighbors to introduce themselves the first day you move in, and arrange a potluck so you can meet the other folks in your neighborhood. It is the invitation to the Women's Club, or the Men's lunch group and the residents' pot lucks, just to get acquainted.

Sunriver spirit is wrapped in the number of volunteers who make things happen around here, from the Citizen Patrol to the Sunriver Music Festival to the Board of Directors to the many committees who give time and effort.

Sunriver spirit surfaced when the entrance sign needed spiffing up, and the Resort, SROA, the Mall and the Rental Managers cooperated to get the job done. Sunriver spirit is there to help folks in need with funds, time and loving thoughts.

We've all come here from somewhere else. We've all *elected* to come here. Perhaps it is this, plus the physical isolation that creates this Sunriver spirit. Perhaps a similar spirit is evident in small communities throughout the world. I like to think so. But those of us from larger cities find it unusual – and we savor it.

BEGINNINGS

By
Dave Ghormley

The day had started out clear and blue. It was cold, and the snow lay heavily on the pasture by the twisting river. Off to the east lay what was left of what the Native People would call Mt. Paulina. Its once towering peak was lying all over the surrounding countryside. The lava was still pouring out of the cauldrons and there was a huge ridge of pure black obsidian forming in the middle. The steam and heat from the bubbling lava was in sharp contrast to the chilly mountainside.

To the west another butte was pushing its way to the top of the horizon. It was the seventh and newest of a series of huge mountains, black and forbidding. The snow melted when it touched the butte, which was still cooling and growing.

A bird flying over Paulina could look off to the northwest and see a line of new buttes pushing up from deep within the earth's crust. One of the largest was erupting violently on this cold, winter day. It was spewing a pall of smoke and ash high into the air, which was beginning to turn day to night. A huge river of lava was flowing from its torn side to the west. The forest burned as the lava pushed through it. The animals tried to scurry off. Too often, they disappeared in a flash of fire.

Suddenly, a great cloud of steam billowed up. The lava had reached the river. As it flowed, it filled the canyon where the river had gouged out its channel over the eons. In no time at all, a great wall of black lava blocked the water, and the river backed up on itself and overflowed its banks.

A huge lake began to form.

In time this lake was over forty miles long. It covered all of the valley. Over the centuries, the silt and topsoil and crushed rock of the surrounding mountains washed down and settled on the lake bed. In spots this sediment went down over 2000 feet. Periodically, another volcanic eruption would occur and gigantic boulders would rain into the lake along with unimaginable tons of ash and dust and small lava particles.

When the lake finally filled, the river cascaded over the lava wall and resumed its relentless trip to the Pacific. Over the years it ate away at the lava, and gradually the wall began to crumble. One day it gave way. The water rushed through. Gradually, the lake drained and the river reestablished its channel at the low spot. However, the sediment had filled in so completely that there was very little difference in the high and the low. There emerged a great, broad plain surrounded by still changing, still active mountains and canyons and lakes and streams.

* * * * *

It was cold and harsh out. The snow came down sideways and the wind lashed through the limbs of the giant ponderosa pine overhead. The family moved instinctively a little closer to the low, glowing fire in the center of the shelter. They knew that the soft, thick elk hides which covered the tepee's frame of strong saplings would keep the wind out and the warmth in, but the cold was so close!

Running Fawn watched from the dark of the outer fringe as the great chief and her father talked. Everything was in readiness for the long, cold winter.

There was a huge cache of dried elk and venison meat, stacks of dried trout and salmon, geese and ducks hanging from the rafters, nuts and berries and native plants dried and cooked and stored away. They had even dredged a bumper crop of wapato root from the bottom of the river, had dried it and ground it. All summer long they had labored to fill their larder. The little meadow lay next to the giant ponderosa and bordered the river, which flowed swift and deep. The elk and the deer, the bear and the cougar, the beaver and the badger and the wolves, the coyotes and the raccoons and the porcupines all went to the river for water each day. Some had stopped to forage in the pasture. Some had felt the bite of her father's arrows, which were made from the obsidian from the sacred mountain, Paulina.

The family and the tribe had lived here for generations. They were part of the Paiute nation. They lived in a hard country, but with care it was a good life. The setting was magnificent. The mountains, the huge forests, the winding river, the occasional pastures and giant outcroppings of huge boulders and lava flows made you catch your breath.

Running Fawn had heard of the high cold lakes in the mountains, deep and clear and full of fish. She had heard it said that at one time the place where she sat had been in a huge lake. Over the years the trees and willows and grasses had invaded the lake bottom. The great flocks of migrating geese and ducks had tarried in the marshes and left seeds and guano, succeeding crops of native grasses had died and added to the humus, the sea animals and the little land animals had died and were covered by the invading plant life.

The earth and its living creatures had found a balance letting them live together in harmony. There were worse places to live and grow old, thought Running Fawn. The drone of the men talking, the fullness she felt from the big meal she had just finished, the whir of the wind through the big old ponderosa, the warmth of the fire made her eyes

6

heavy. She drifted off into the deep sleep of the child. She was safe and secure.

* * * * * *

"You know," said the red-faced mountain man to anyone who would listen, "I don't think anyone could make a living in this country! It's too cold and the growing season is just too short. Look at the soil! It's sandy and has no nutrition. All this country is good for is to grow pine trees. However, I will admit it's good at that. Man, look at these big old ponderosas. Some must be hundreds of years old."

Lieutenant Henry Abbot was inclined to agree. He was following the footsteps of John Fremont, who had passed through this country in 1843 and now the army wanted the area surveyed. He and his party arrived at the great old ponderosa beside the pasture in September, 1855. It was a good place to set up camp and from which to work for a week or two.

The men had been struggling through a forest of giant ponderosas. The huge trees shaded out the underbrush, so it had not been too hard to make their way, but it was easy to get lost and depressing to always be in the shade of the big trees. He was glad to be out in the sun beside the pasture.

They set up camp and one of the men went down to a nearby marsh. In a few minutes they could hear his musket, and he soon returned with a brace of big Canada geese for their dinner. Another man came in with freshly caught trout. Soon the smell of the cooking fowl and fish filled the campsite.

While waiting for the dinner to be prepared, Lt. Abbot kicked idly in the dusty soil under the tree. In no time he'd uncovered a handful of obsidian which had been chipped from a larger piece. There were even arrowheads and crude obsidian cutting knives among the chips. This old tree had

7

seen many before him, he reflected.

"Chow's on!," cried the cook. Abbot sauntered over to the campfire and loaded his mess kit with mouth watering food.

The lieutenant sat down against the big old ponderosa and ate while enjoying the sight of the sun dropping behind the mountain which loomed up in the distance. He'd had worse assignments.

* * * * *

Jeremy Todd was hot and frustrated and hungry. All morning long he had been poking among the jack pines and the willows looking for those three stray heifers. Whenever he got close, he'd hear them crash off in a new direction, and there was nothing he and his horse, Abbie, could do to head them off and get them started back towards the big field. He knew that they were about ready to calve, and he wanted them behind fences in the main pasture today so that the calves would be safe and healthy before they disappeared with their mothers back into the brush.

Jeremy and Abbie came to the little pasture over near the river. The heat waves were shimmering up from the land, and the flies were buzzing. It was one thing to be thought of as an experienced cowpoke. It was quite another to be a hungry twelve year old at lunchtime. The heifers could wait!

Jeremy tossed Abbie's reins over her head and watched as she started to graze in the waist high mountain grass. He reached in the saddlebag and pulled out a jug of water and the big, thick meat sandwich his mother had handed him as he left the ranch that morning. He squatted down under a big old tree and bit into the juicy beef.

When he had finished eating, Jeremy slouched on his back for a few minutes, thinking. His dad had homesteaded here a few years ago, and the home ranch was down by the big meadow. He knew his daddy and the hired hand were out scything fresh mountain grass for the hay pile. His mom and sisters had a full day of work ahead because the berries were ripe on the vines and there was a rush to get the fresh vegetables cooked and into storage.

His older brother, Tim, and his friend, Gus, were up in the mountains where most of the herd was grazing on the tender new grass up there. He envied them. He had wanted to go, too. He knew that they'd camp out in a good spot near one of those great deep mountain lakes tonight. They'd get plenty of fishing in and would probably bring back an elk or a deer on the packhorse.

But here he was, chasing some stupid heifers who didn't have sense enough to know that they'd better head on into the big pasture if they didn't want a cougar or a wolf to get their calves. Where in the dickens had those heifers gone? Jeremy knew enough about cattle to guess that they were probably holed up in the willows keeping cool and shaded. They'd eaten their fill this morning and were probably lying down chewing their cuds and laughing at him by now.

He whistled at Abbie, and the little mare perked up her ears and trotted over.

Jeremy couldn't help but smile. She liked this nice warm weather just like he did. Even though it was a pain to be chasing these ornery critters, it was better than sitting in that one-room schoolhouse over at the Vandevert Ranch next door and then having to pick his way back home through a blizzard in time to go do chores before dark. Abbie liked this better, too.

Jeremy heard a lowing sound followed by a deep cough over in the willows next to the river. There they were! He vaulted onto Abbie and they went scurrying across the pasture. The heifers struggled up reluctantly and began to run. This time, they were running in the direction of the main pasture. Now, he'd get them home.

The breeze blew through his hair and rushed by as they galloped. The big old ponderosa and the little pasture and the river were left in the dust.

* * * * *

"Let's go on one last picnic over by the river," suggested Mabel Schoenquist. "It will never be the same after the army gets through with it. I don't know whether we'll ever be back, but I'll bet if we do return, everything will look different- and not for the better."

"You're right," her husband, Frank, responded. "I don't know of a nicer place anywhere than under that big old tree over there. They'll probably chop it down and use it to make a bridge or something. I just hate to see that happen.

In an hour they were all piled into the wagon and the team of horses pulled away from the ranch house and headed down the lane towards the river. The team seemed to know just where to go, and probably did, when you think of all the times they had hauled them over there.

It was one of those fresh June days. The sun beat down. The red-winged blackbirds were calling, the doves were answering, it seemed like. A crazy old gray squirrel ran across the path in front of them and scurried up a lodge pole pine. He chattered crossly at them as they glided by.

When they arrived at the pasture, the kids headed for the river. They had a favorite tree over across the bend where they had rigged up a long rawhide rope. It had knots every two or three feet and made a great swing for them as they swung far out over the river and splashed in with great shouts of glee.

Mabel unpacked their lunch under the big old ponderosa while Frank unhitched the horses and hobbled them.

10

He tied a feed bag on each and watched as they swatted flies off their rumps with their long tails.

"You know, Mabel, this place has been awfully good to us. We'll miss it."

"Well, I could stand some electricity and a store a little closer than fifteen miles and some neighbors to talk to once in awhile."

"I know. It may be fancier where we're going, and we can't gripe about what the Army paid us for the place. Couldn't have asked for any more. And all in cash on the barrelhead. Nice to do business with Uncle Sam. But even so, I'm not sure we'll find any other place any nicer. This is hard to beat."

Mabel nodded. "Can you imagine this place something other than a cattle spread? An Army camp! Won't those soldier boys be lonely, though! I still don't understand how they can make sense out of turning this place into a training camp. It's about as far out in the weeds as you can get. What are they trying to hide?"

"They tell that they are going to train the guys in how to build bridges across a river to get ready for the invasion of Germany. Can you imagine? I would think that the Rhine would be a damned sight tougher to cross than the Deschutes! If they want to build bridges, why not build them where people can use them after they're through! Sounds crazy to me." Frank shook his head.

"Come on, kids! Time to eat," Mabel shouted. "Gee, Frank, I am going to miss this old tree and that pretty little meadow and that view across the river at old Bachelor Butte. You're right. We'll have to go some to find a better place, even if we do have electricity there!"

* * * * *

"Man! Do I have some good news!"

11

The squad had been huddled over a small fire near the big old ponderosa. The rain was coming down and the pasture in front of them was a sea of mud where the tanks had been maneuvering and the anti-tank barriers were scattered about.

Down next to the river was a big pile of logs which had come in from the forest that morning. The squad had just piled it up and was getting ready to build another floating bridge across the river. How many of these damned things did they have to build before that stupid bird colonel had had enough? What a turkey!

"What's the word, Jasper?" The corporal asked.

Every squad had its gossip, and Jasper was theirs. He always heard the rumors before the rest of them. The nice thing was that he was generally right.

"All right! Listen up! You're not going to believe this! We've been ordered out. We're being sent to Ft. Lewis up near Tacoma! ASAP, yet. How about that!"

"I don't believe it," grunted the corporal. "Even the army wouldn't screw up that bad. Hell, we just got here a couple of years ago. We just finished building that damned officer's club. They've only had one party in it. They won't pull out that fast!"

"Oh, yeah? Just you wait."

And Jasper was right. But then, so was the corporal.

In no time at all the first two-thirds of the camp personnel were up in Ft. Lewis, pulling liberty in Olympia aand Tacoma and Seattle. But Jasper's squad was still trying to get into Bend on the weekends and still had to sing as they marched and still had to sweat and slave the hours away. The only difference was that they were tearing down Camp Abbot rather than building it. The rows of sickening green barracks were gone. The anti-tank barriers were history. The parade

12

grounds and the mess hall and the garages and the offices and the sickbay and the jail were destroyed.

Pretty soon all that was left was the Officer's Club and the sewer plant and rows of cement foundations and surplus logs and pilings from all the bridge building. No one was about to tear down that officers club after all the sweat and misery that went into building it. Every man in the battalion had cursed it when it was going up. Dead cold weather, slippery logs being hoisted into place by "slave" labor, a hated colonel who kept driving them until they would have gladly dropped a log on his head, and the whole idea of the place being there for the officers with no woman within an hour's drive! What did they need it for! May it rot in hell. Not one of them would even consider taking it down. It didn't even show on the master plans. No one in the Pentagon would ever know. To hell with it! Let's get out of here.

After months of undoing what had been done, the squad loaded up on a 5 by 5 and convoyed off to the North. They gave Bend a Bronx Cheer as they went through town. If they never saw that place again, it would be too soon!

* * * * *

Lee Evans was an Oklahoma wildcatter. He was an outdoorsman and knew what it was to take a chance. He didn't know a darned thing about developing land, but he knew that land could be good to you.

One day a relative, who was a big rancher and lumberman in Eastern Oregon, spotted him in a bar and asked him to come on over for a drink. It turned out that the guy had a bit of a problem. He had a cash-flow problem. He was having trouble meeting his payroll. If Lee could loan him some money, he'd put up an old ranch he owned down south of Bend as collateral.

To make a long story short, in due course, Lee ended up

13

with the deed to the ranch. Now what was he supposed to do with it?

He contacted a fellow by the name of Don McCallum, who was head of a big land title company in Portland. Mac was interested. He and his wife, Mary, took a drive over to Bend and went down and checked the old ranch out. Instead of a ranch, they found the remains of a military base! There were weeds growing out of the red lava cinder roads, weeds growing around the abandoned cement footings of buildings, weeds around the old entrance barricade. Sitting out in the middle of all this weed patch and junk pile was the old Officer's Club. Intriguing!

They looked around at all of the property. The weeds had grown back into the parade ground. The pilings in the river over near a beautiful pasture told of the floating bridges which had been there a few years ago. The old cement sewer plant tanks sat forlornly in the center of what had been at the end of the cantonment area, and were too sturdy to be demolished by anything less than an atom bomb.

But the natural beauty of the place shown through. They wandered beside the river and had a picnic under a big old ponderosa tree and looked at Bachelor Butte looming up beyond the little pasture, framed by the river and a beautiful grove of big trees. They fell in love with it all. They came home enthused. So, they made a deal with Evans and became part owners. It wasn't long after this that they decided that if they were going to do anything with the property, they needed more financial horsepower than they could provide. John Gray, a successful manufacturing executive in Portland, had just completed Salishan on the Oregon Coast. The McCallums were charmed with what had been done there, and they felt that there was a good chance for the same kind of development in Central Oregon. They intro-

14

uced John Gray to the property, and, soon, he was a part owner, too.

They all went to work with a vengeance. Lee Evans sat in the corner and took in all of these meetings and plans and projections.

One day, he said, "I'm in over my head. This is a lot more ambitious than I had in mind. If this is what you all want to do, I'd like you to buy me out."

In due course, they did just that. The stage was set for the development of Sunriver. They brought in a team of land planners, including Bob Royston from the Bay Area, who seemed to have a lot to do with the first plans. He and the other planners and the partners, of course, defined the first concept for the land.

The original idea of Sunriver was that a series of small villages would be constructed, joined together by winding trails. There was even talk of just using bikes and golf carts for transportation. Each village would be unique and isolated, enveloped in the woods and fields and ponds, close to Nature's animals and bird life. A touch of heaven safely tucked away in the piney woods.

It didn't quite work out that way. Economics got in the way. But many of the principles that underlay this original plan are still with us in abundance.

Today there are monuments to the past aplenty. Mary McCallum Park is our "owners park", and is a fitting memorial to one of our early visionaries. The Great Hall is a monument to the sweat, blood, and tears of the soldiers. There is a little log cabin that used to be a line refuge for the cowboys.

But best of all, the little meadow by the river and the big old ponderosa with all those obsidian fragments buried near its roots still is there in the sun and the snow. It has always been a treasured place.

As I sit here under that ancient, wonderful tree and look across the meadow at the river and the mountains and the forest, all I can say is, " May this always be a treasured place."

Dave Ghormley

* * * * * *

SUNRIVER GEESE

By
Keith S. Pennington

There was once a goose on the thirteenth tee

Who flew wingman in the Perfect Vee

But since he couldn't dodge a golf ball

Geese trumpets now record his fall

As they fly in an unbalanced Vee

Annis Oetinger

MEMORIES OF SUNRIVER

By
Annis Oetinger

Sunriver sounded like a place we'd like to see. We had just moved from England to a small town in Illinois. Having been born and raised in Oregon, we felt as if we really needed a foothold on the Far-west land. When you've grown up with the Oregon scenery and life style, it's hard to get very excited about Illinois. If you've seen one corn field, you've seen them all.

On our first trip back West, we started looking for property and ended up with Meadow House 81. The view along the 17th fairway of the Meadows course toward the hills beyond enchanted us. Each year we managed at least a couple of trips to our "little gray home in the West".

As I write this, Christmas is just over for 1997, and I find my memories turn to Christmases we spent here since 1973. The pictures start with Mother, Father and three children. Some years the snow was deep, other years it was non-existent. Sometimes other friends or relatives joined us, and after a few years two grandchildren shared the fun. Always there was a special mystique about Christmas in Sunriver.

Usually we found time to be here for a visit in the summer too. We measured the growth of the community year by year. The Lodge and Great Hall were central. At first, the commercial facilities consisted of just the service station with a small convenience store and post office where Marcello's is now. It was a major development when the grocery store built a new home and became a supermarket. The shops in the board-walk area of the mall and some

17

offices plus a bigger post office added to the town. Meanwhile new homes and condos sprouted up all through the south end and spread on up the hill to the north.

The north golf course, now Woodlands, was laid out, and by this time we had decided Sunriver was our place to retire. One Christmas we purchased a lot on the Woodlands 7th hole, and started to daydream about the home we'd build there. Each month we eagerly looked forward to the various Sunriver publications to keep us informed about what was going on in our home-to-be.

Each time we came for a visit, it was hard to leave. When we had to turn our faces east, our feet dragged. From our car or airplane window, we'd watch the lovely scenery slip away. Goodbye to the mountains, the forests and rivers. One year as we drove east, we passed a car with an Oregon license plate heading east also. Our younger son looked out the window in disbelief.

"What's he going that way for? Go back, go back!"

A SUNRIVER MYTH

by
Keith S. Pennington

Thousands and thousands of days ago, near the dawn of time for Sunriver (which makes it about 1969); the fogs lifted from the primordial valley revealing a scene of splendor. Deer grazed contentedly in this beautiful valley carved out by the ice age glaciers as they receded northward (this was a little before 1969).

Groves of Ponderosa pine dotted the floor of the valley providing food and refuge for the numerous squirrels, chipmunks and other members of the rodent family that darted hither and yon across the valley floor; sometimes stopping to rush headlong up the trees and across the quivering branches. The porcupine lumbered slowly across the terrain, frequently pausing to nibble on the bark of trees and ruin the day for some saplings that had dreams of someday being giant Ponderosa. The coyotes occasionally ran across the glades, suspiciously checking in all directions for predators and prey.

It was to this scene of pastoral beauty that mankind came, bringing his front-end loaders, power saws, hammers, nails and power staplers. They looked around and said "Wow! This is real neat!". At that the valley rang out with the rhythmic beats of hammers and pneumatic staplers which intermingled with the melodies of the song birds, random cawing of the crows and the raucous trumpeting of the geese relaying flight information as they winged their way across this valley which was to become known as "Sunriver- -the Central Oregon and West Coast resort destination of choice".

In the early days, mankind slowly moved across the rregion now known as Sunriver, building houses and cabins. It was during the early days of this settlement that a man named Mr. D. del Us came to this paradise. It was widely rumored that he was a descendent of the ancient Greek inventor Daedalus, of labyrinthine fame. Soon after arriving in the area Mr. D. del Us was appointed to the site planning committee that was assembled to develop the area as a resort with the capabilities of attracting tourists from all over the world. With his clearly inherited capabilities as an inventor and designer, he rapidly moved ahead, finally becoming the chief planner of the area. The plans for a lodge and golf courses proceeded apace and slowly the first small numbers of tourists arrived in the area to sample the many pleasures that were available in the Sunriver area. However, it was at about this same time that another type of traveler was to arrive on the Sunriver scene. These travelers were far more numerous,tended to stay very briefly in the environs of Sunriver and rarely satisfied the goals of the Sunriver Association and residents. These goals of course had little to do with money. No! They had a lot to do with money! These brief and fleeting tourists were considered to be the scourge of mankind and came to be derisively known by the name Mini-tour; which was derived from the Greek word Minotaur; a creature much disliked by the ancient residents of Crete.

After several heated meetings the Sunriver Association ordered D. del Us to find a way to keep these Mini-tours from escaping the area. To which he agreed, but said in a low and barely discernible voice "Where have I heard this before?" That evening he went home and pulled out the family albums searching for inspiration, when all of a sudden it came to him: He would take the Sunriver Associations request as a challenge for him to exceed even the renown of his ancient relative who had become enormously famous by merely constructing that puny excuse for a labyrinth on Crete. So he immediately set to work on designing a system of roads, streets and alleys that would entrap these Mini-tours in a manner far more elaborate than that of his well known predecessor. It is now well known that he greatly exceeded his ancestor in both design and complexity. The system of circles and roads that he designed, combined with directional signs that are either too numerous to read or far too small for even the eagles to read first time around, must be consider a stroke of genius. To the delight of the Sunriver Association, this ingenious maze that he constructed in Sunriver was instrumental in significantly slowing down the escape of all Mini-tours and it is rumored that some were so frustrated in their efforts to escape that they broke down and bought houses. Many who were caught in this group of home buyers were the result of Mr. D. del Us's ingenious scheme for providing for the needs of Mini-tours that arrived at night— that is, he didn't!!

But the major, and crowning glory that is attributed to this modern day designer of labyrinths and mazes, is something that far surpasses the capabilities of his glorious ancestor Daedalus. Although he has not yet achieved the fame of his ancient ancestor, as time unfolds he will almost definitely achieve ultimate glory. In this regard, there is no doubt that his contribution to the art of labyrinths, namely as a series of roads connected to a system of circles numbered up to eleven but then intentionally omitting circle eight, was brilliant. Even if the Mini-tours had a ball of string to assist them in escaping from this maze they were all caught off guard by this ingenious use of numbers.

It is clear that Mr. D. del Us deserves the credit for this

final numerically deceiving addition to the labyrinthine art. Through this intricate maze he has been able to provide for some of the fondest and most frustrating memories of Sunriver for those few Mini-tours fortunate enough to escape.

Lest anyone doubt the contributions of Mr. D. del Us during his stay in Sunriver, it might be wise to take into consideration my recent experience while riding on the bike trails—another of Mr.D. del Us's contributions. While following orange, green and blue trails that were marked with like colored arrows to guide the uninitiated, I noted that the directional arrows had been either painted over or covered up by another layer of asphalt at critical junctions. The results of this small addition by D. del Us to the overall Sunriver plan was ingenious. It resulted in numerous Mini-tours, who had actually found their way to their rental home the night before, gathering in crowds and gazing hopelessly at maps which purported to decipher the overall design while at the same time attempting to stay upright on their bikes and also control the wanderings of all of their mini-Mini-tours. Further down the trail I happened across a rather disheveled person who was attempting to hang onto a cart taken from the Market. Feeling his sense of total helplessness, I stopped and asked if I could help. He then told me that he had arrived in Sunriver in 1988 and had been wandering around since trying to get out. Apparently he had managed to follow the roads as far as circle seven and had then become totally lost trying to get to circle eight. He begged and pleaded with me on bended knee to show him the way out of Sunriver. His was, no doubt, a very unfortunate case, made more so by the fact that I had to inform him that my wife and I had arrived in Sunriver a few months earlier and we had finally given up and bought a home just off circle six.

Since the departure of Mr. D. del Us from Sunriver the

Design Review Committee has vowed to keep his memory alive, and although they concede that they can never hope to match the subtlety and sheer complexity of his design, they have committed to rewrite the Sunriver Specifications and Design Recommendations in a manner worthy of his memory. It should be noted that some residents, no doubt trapped ex-Mini-tours, have suggested that they had already surpassed this goal.

As a footnote it should be said that we are often asked what happened to Mr. D. del Us after he left Sunriver. Although nothing specific is known about his later years, it was widely understood that he had taken a high level position at the Internal Revenue Service where he proceeded to further refine the labyrinthine art; applying his findings to the writing of forms and schedules. More recently, however, he was reported to have been seen in the company of lawyers assembled near the Supreme Court.

* * * * * *

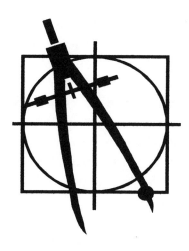

MUSIC AMONG THE PINES

By
DC Born

Sunriver was younger then. There were fewer houses, fewer cars, fewer people. But the forest was plentiful and the mountains stood tall above the fairways and beyond that little stream for which the community is named - Sun River. And, for a few nights in August, the sound of music echoed among the pines.

The year was 1978. After nearly two years of planning, the Sunriver Music Festival debuted in this idyllic setting. That inaugural concert season consisted of three sold-out evenings of chamber music performed by an ensemble of 28 players under the direction of Maestro Lawrence Leighton Smith. Featured were a flute recital by Festival co-founder Ray Fabrizio and the World Premiere of Gordon Playman's composition: Quintet.

The inspiration of creating a music festival in Sunriver was the result of a visit by Fabrizio to the rustic Great Hall in the company of his former California neighbors, Polly and Doug Kahle. Standing together beneath the vaulted wooden ceiling of this historic log structure, these friends envisioned a musical "happening" which, over the succeeding years, has been called Central Oregon's "best event of the summer."

A distinguished steering committee was formed. The developer of Sunriver - and owner of the Resort - agreed to provide the Great Hall. Maestro Smith, then Conductor of the Oregon Symphony, agreed to be the Festival's first Artistic Director and Conductor. And, as they say, the rest is history. It's a history of much hard work, the inevitable several hands full of difficulties, and a continuum of re-

sounding artistic successes. It's a history of dedicated volunteers and outstanding musicians working together to provide
season after season of captivating performances. And, within
this history of sustained commitment to providing outstanding classical music to Central Oregon, there also was a history
of adjustment and change.

In addition to its orchestra of talented musicians, the
Festival has enjoyed the artistic skills of quite a number of
renowned soloists as well as guest conductors, the latter
including James DePreist, the current Music Director and
Conductor of the Oregon Symphony.

However, over the Festival's 21 seasons (through the
concerts of August 1998), only two persons have filled the
position of Artistic Director and Conductor. Maestro Smith,
now Professor of Conducting and Conductor-in-Residence
of the Yale School of Music, was the first, serving the Festival
through the 1982 season.

Sung Kwak, Music Director of the Austin Symphony,
was the Festival's second Artistic Director and Conductor.
One of four guest conductors for the '83 season, his term
began with the '84 season and continued through the 1993
season. For the '94 season, Maestro Smith returned to the
Festival and continues to the present.

With the Festival's incorporation in 1979, a Board of
Directors was established to oversee the events and conduct
fund raising efforts. Bruce Bischof was elected president.
Through the 1998 season, 10 distinguished persons have
held that position, Sybil Gibson taking the honors for
longevity, serving three terms.

During 1987-88, the Festival was re-organized to its
current configuration, the responsibilities of the original
board being divided between a Board of Trustees and a
Volunteer Council. In 1988, Kate Hannon was hired as

full-time Executive Director, replacing and expanding the position of Managing Director held by Jim Reeves since the Festival's beginning.

As a result of extensive yearly membership campaigns led by the Festival's current Executive Director, Gail Mitchell, the number of corporate sponsors and private members experienced significant growth over the past few years (less than 200 prior to 1995 to over 500 in 1997). Also, the advent of the Festival Faire and the availability of StoneRidge Townhomes to facilitate an expanded winter-time concert series called Fireside Concerts have proven to be major income producers. Together, these activities helped return the Festival to a strong financial footing in 1996.

In addition to offering the concert series each August, the Festival has been particularly active in providing classical music opportunities to the youth of Central Oregon. Over the years, there have been children's concerts, the Youth Institute for Strings, Master Classes and Workshops (supported by scholarships), and the Young Artists Scholarship program which was begun in 1996 with a grant from the Sunriver Women's Club.

In the "Twentieth Season Book," the Festival's historians, Mary and Gerry Sawyer, state: "The Festival has a solid record of success since its founding, having become a major community event...."

The community of Sunriver and the Festival have, in many ways, grown up together. And as is true of the community itself, the Festival has both changed and stayed much the same. While the number of houses has increased, as have the cars and people, the basic quality and character of the community remains. The forest still is plentiful and the mountains still stand tall above the airways and beyond that little stream for which the community is named.

Likewise, the Festival. The August concerts still are held in the Great Hall, now courtesy of the Resort's new owners. And while the Festival's budget and membership and fund-raisers and number of volunteers have increased, the quality of the music that echoes through the pines each August remains as magnificent as was envisioned by Frabrizio and the Kahles when they first walked together beneath the arched ceiling and rugged chandeliers of the Great Hall way back in 1976.

CIRCLE EIGHT

By
Keith S. Pennington

There was once a lady from Detroit Lake

Who came to Sunriver by mistake

Going to Bachelor one day

She got lost on the way

And is still trying to find Circle Eight

IT TAKES A WISE MAN

By
Mel Johnson

Men of Sunriver, it is a common belief that golf can be a family affair where husbands and wives join in playful communion in beautiful surroundings on fairways and greens, congratulating the good shot and commiserating over a stroke of bad luck - a joyful experience. It can be that and more, but there is a dark side lurking in wait before that ultimate condition is attained. The moment of truth arrives when the wife first asks the husband to teach her to play golf. Should that happen to you, run, don't walk to the nearest teaching pro, and beg him to take her off your hands.

On a danger scale of one to ten, with one being feeding cookies to a spotted fawn and ten being comparable to circumcising a wolverine, teaching your wife to play golf is at least an eleven. Many an affectionate, loving relationship has been wrecked without hope of redemption by a few ill-chosen words from the well-intentioned husband while trying to correct some minor flaw in his wife's backswing. All male golfers should be aware that they are treading a thin line between instruction and offense where one careless word can release an unbridled fury in the most gentle of wives.

This peculiarity was demonstrated to me several years ago when I was witness to the peril involved. It happened on a municipal course where I used to play a couple of times a week. This day we were invited to play with Paul and his new wife who was being introduced to the game for the very first time. She appeared to be charming, mild-mannered and eager to learn. They seemed to be a devoted couple as he politely adjusted her grip and stance and applauded vigorously at each practice swing. I stood by and marveled as he patiently instructed her in the fundamentals — straight left arm, eyes on the ball, slow back swing, don't look up — all the basics.

Called to the tee, she strode confidently to the ball, took a deliberate backswing with perfect form, and lunged wildly, topping the ball, which dribbled barely thirty feet. Paul smiled and cautioned her not to worry, such things happen to everybody. He calmly reviewed the fundamentals once more and sent her back to the ball. Eight swings and eight topped balls later, we arrived at the first green.

Spurred by shouts coming from back on the tee, we hurried to the second hole where Paul nervously renewed the coaching of his even more nervous wife. The second hole was a repeat of the first. Scuffed balls and shanks continued as we began letting other foursomes play through. To her credit, Paul's wife desperately tried to follow his instruction, but to no avail.

By the time we reached the fourth tee, we noticed that Paul's voice was rising to a near shout, and his face was turning crimson. Doggedly, he warned her not to look up and not to collapse the left arm, but the results were always the same. Divots the size of Big Macs were ripped from the fairways, and the nightmare dragged on endlessly as passing foursomes glared at us when we moved aside to let them play through.

The struggling couple had lapsed into a strained silence by the time we reached the eighth hole, a long par five. Following her usual botched drive, Paul's voice rose to a bellow heard all over the front nine. He completely lost it as he launched into a tirade, and foremost among his ill-chosen statements was the word "dumb".

At that, the wife burst into tears, threw her driver into some bushes and stomped off down the fairway, never looking back. Paul was left standing, ashen-faced, staring skyward, realizing that he had just double-bogeyed his marriage. After several moments, he dejectedly retrieved the driver, shouldered both golf bags and followed his wife down the fairway, a picture of remorse and regret.

After completing the ninth, we both agreed that we had had enough golf for the day, and since Paul was stranded five miles from home, I offered to drop him off. He was a pitiful sight going up to his front door looking like a condemned man going to his execution. In my imagination I could picture the ugly scene about to unfold.

We didn't see much of Paul after that. A few months later his name appeared in the local newspaper as a statistic in the divorce column. He would rarely appear on the golf course, playing alone, usually just nine holes. He then spent the rest of the afternoon in the bar - a lonely, broken man and an object lesson to any man who may be tempted to try to teach his wife to play the demanding game of golf.

Here in Sunriver we are blessed with three magnificent golf courses and all the amenities including staffs of trained professional instructors waiting to relieve you of the stress and potential danger lying in wait for one careless word in a moment of distress. Do not expose yourself to the tragic fate of my friend, Paul. Enjoy the superb golf and beautiful weather, and leave the driving to others. Patience and understanding will reward you with a delightful playing partner and increase your enjoyment of the wonderful challenge of golf.

SASQUATCH IN SUNRIVER
By

Kathie Thatcher

Numerous Bigfoot sightings have been reported in the Central Oregon area in the last few months;. The first came from a hunter in the LaPine area last fall. He told the Deschutes County Sheriff's Office that he had caught a fleeting glimpse of a large, hairy humanoid accompanied by an almost overwhelming stench.

The creature resurfaced early this month in the Sunriver Mall. He first appeared at the back door of the Dough Factory early one morning frightening owner Don Limbocker. Hoping to appease him, Limbocker offered a freshly baked Bigfoot doughnut. However the creature indicated a preference for one of the bakery's "Spare Tires".

Later that morning the Sasquatch entered Mr. T's Video and asked to rent a movie, "Harry and the Hendersons". According to the manager, Jackie Bue, the movie was already reserved for that evening. She later told investigating police that she probably wouldn't have rented to him anyway. Said Bue, "We require a major credit card for all new customers, and I sure as heck didn't see any pockets in all that fur."

Jim Bergeron of Pacific Crest Clothing also reported a visit from Sasquatch. He was annoyed because the creature's odor drove the other customers from the store. Nevertheless, he attempted to find him a suitable article of clothing. Unfortunately, he had nothing to offer in an XXXXL Tall. Although the visitor was disappointed in the limited sizes carried in the store, he seemed to be pleased with the large selection of natural fibers. Bergeron commented, "His feet really aren't all that large."

Another sighting was reported later that afternoon at Village Properties by rental manager, Linda Longstreet. Bigfoot stated that he was looking for a short term rental, something with a very large hot tub and a rustic décor. Longstreet said that at this point his aroma was beginning to make her feel faint so she suggested they continue the interview outside. When she tried to discuss payment, including a rather substantial pet deposit, the customer seemed confused and abruptly left.

When Mall owner, Joe Weston, was questioned by this reporter about the type of clientele he is currently trying to attract to the Mall his response was a brusque, "No comment".

There are conflicting reports that the creature in question was seen drinking at P.J.B.'s Restaurant and Lounge in the Sunriver Business Park. When questioned, the bartender replied, "I dunno. I suppose he coulda been here. We get a lotta big hairy guys in this place, and some of them are pretty ripe."

Final evidence of the creature's presence in the area occurred the following day when the owner of Spacemaker Storage, in the Sunriver Business Park, Sidney Reynolds, noticed a foul odor emanating from one of her vacant units and some unusual tracks entering and leaving. Investigating officers did not discover the big-footed interloper, but they did find evidence of recent occupation: some large hairballs, a few fleas and a rough bed made of bitterbrush branches.

The snowy tracks led to the temporary library at Crossroads Center where the book drop appeared to have been tampered with. The library later reported that a book with references to Sasquatch was missing. No further sightings have been reported since the first of the month.

Jay Bowerman, naturalist and Director Emeritus of the Sunriver Nature Center shed some additional light on the sightings. Bowerman, a local expert, has taught classes titled "In Pursuit of the Elusive Sasquatch". In 1974 he made a cast of a large print embedded in the mud along the banks of the Deschutes River near our community. He describes Sasquatch as between 7 and 8 feet in height, weighing up to 300 pounds.

Normally it is spotted in forested areas. Why would it show up in Sunriver? Replies Bowerman, "Well, this is a Tree City."

He concluded our interview by remarking that the creature reportedly is highly intelligent and curious. It might well be interested in a community such as ours which exists so closely in turn with nature. He added that Sasquatch might consider his appearances here as a good joke on the human population.

CHRISTENING THE PRINCESS

By
DC Born

The day could not have been more beautiful nor more appropriate for the occasion. Warm, brilliantly sunny, uplifting of one's spirits. Just the conditions for an enjoyable outing in the great outdoors. Then I had to go and spoil it by proving the axiom that stupidity is a self-inflicted condition.

It was late morning when Rita and I arrived at the marina and put our shiny new blue Princess canoe in the water. Rita proudly took her place in the bow where, all prim and proper like a real-life Monet sans parasol, she waited for me to board so we could begin our maiden voyage. The floating dock bobbed with exaggerated oscillations as I prepared to take my place in the waiting craft. Confidently, I stepped in, sure that all was well with the world.

But it wasn't, a condition which instantly was apparent as I found myself waist-deep in river water, transfixed with a confusion that soon would turn into red-faced embarrassment. Rita, too, was in the water. She, too, was shocked and a bit confused. Having had her back to me, she'd had no idea what was about to transpire until she felt herself being dumped. And worse than merely being wet and embarrassed, she couldn't touch bottom. After Rita finally secured a tenuous hold on the dock, our first maneuver was to salvage our belongings, all of which had joined us in the drink.

My next objective was to try salvaging my dignity. And that really became a most significant issue when I realized that our little escapade was the noontime entertainment of the luncheon crowd at the Trout House. Dignity became an even more pronounced objective when a young waitress came from the restaurant to see if she could help. With a feeble smile, I said thanks but that we were fine and could recover. My feigned bravado didn't seem to impress the woman. But she soon gave up offering assistance and hurried back to her "paying" customers.

The canoe finally was sufficiently emptied of water so we could get the heck out of there. With wet clothes pasted on our backs and wet smiles on our faces, Rita and I waved to our audience as we hurriedly paddled away from the dock with a nonchalance neither of us felt.

The whole episode took less than ten minutes. The memory of the christening of our Princess will long remain.

* * * * * *

SPEED

By
Keith S. Pennington

Driving on East and West Cascade

Watch out for Sunriver's Brigade

If you drive twenty-six

You can get into a fix

So good luck with your Legal Aid!

POLICE LOG

By
DC Born/RC Antle

It seems that a favorite literary item of Sunriver residents, at least those who read the SCENE - is the Police Log. Each month the Log is one of the first columns read, it being a compendium of incidents and complaints, arrests and warnings regarding a vast variety of goings-on in Sunriver about which most of us would otherwise not be aware. And on top of that, it often is amusing.

Although most folks probably think that crime and mischief could not possibly be much of a factor of life in this community of law abiding citizens, it turns out that the job of maintaining law and order has its moments. Some are quite serious, others rather humorous, each one unique, to say the least. But it also turns out that even for the serious stuff the officers who write the Police Log try diligently to put a "smiley face" on it.

Here are a few examples of the "all-in-a-day's-work" efforts of our officers.

o Pit bull got in fight with porcupine. Loaned pliers to pull out quills. Owner happy; dog was not.

o Six teenagers loudly telling scary stories to each other in the dark. Advised they were disturbing the peace.

o Two minors asking people (including security officer) to buy beer for them in Country Store.

o Noise complaint. Officer discovered guests having a party on the back deck, dining in the nude. Told to turn down music and put on clothes.

o Golf-ball retriever stolen from vehicle at Woodlands course. Three sets of golf clubs and other valuables overlooked. Retriever found in another vehicle broken into.

o Subjects camping at Marina with tent and camp fire. Packed up and moved on.

o Renters unable to disarm alarm. Rental agency had not given renter disarming code because agency did not know house had alarm. Owner did not know house had alarm. Discovered house had been pre-wired. Unplugged alarm. It did not disable alarm. Pulled wires from siren. Siren disarmed. Owner advised.

o Fire across from Siskin Lane was contained at less than one acre because homeowner ferried firefighters across river in his boat to get to the fire.

o Two adult males driving a Lodge golf cart in front of the Police Station were stopped and cited for using the cart for something other than what it was rented for.

o Lost seeing-eye dog. Last seen in Lodge area.

o Swarm of bees entered closet. Told to shoo; they did not. Advised to seek help from pest control.

o Airhorn heard at 1 a.m. Train parked near owners storage lot, north end. Airhorn stuck, fixed and train moved on.

o Two 14-yr-olds caught in center of Circle 3 smoking a bong. Boys released to parents, bong destroyed.

o Residents reported strange noises from garage area. Located signs of raccoons feasting from garbage cans.

o Two juveniles sneaking around bushes, Circle 6, having water balloon fight with friends. (They lost).

o Rescued 10 baby ducks from in front of Hot Peppers restaurant; injured mother had taken flight. Babies taken to Nature Center for care.

o Complaint about dog "doing his business" in front of Post Office - and others stepping in his "business."

o Toyota 4-Runner slipped into river while owner was

getting his boat. Assisted tow truck in moving boulders so it could get close enough to river to remove Toyota.

o Night golf game on Meadows course. All 18 groups [sic] drunk, making noise, running around with tiki torches; claimed they had permission.

o Noise complaint. Public Works grinding tree limbs. Owner thought it was too early to be working since most people don't get out of bed until at least 8:30.

And our very favorite from the Summer of '97 -

o Dead animal, possible calf elk, spotted floating in water near stables. ODFW advised to pop belly and let sink. Stables worker shot belly with .22 cal pistol. Animal floated down stream.

We shall never know where this critter finally ended, or, for that matter, any of the myriad details of the hundreds of other items found in our monthly ration of the Police Log. Suffice it to say that the diversity of "things" our officers face never ceases to amaze, nor the diligence and delicacy with which they accomplish the job. We appreciate it all. And most definitely, the humor!

* * * * * *

*   Taken from the Police Log in the Sunriver Scene.

TO GRAMMIE'S HOUSE

By
Mary Ellen Anderson

The most welcome words you can hear as you wait for your children and grandchildren to arrive are "They're here!" Here being Sunriver, and what a beautiful place to be.

Our thirteen grandchildren and four sets of parents have been coming here for seventeen years, all at the same time for two weeks of exciting and fun-filled vacation. It is amazing how each child marks his or her growing up in Sunriver – it's a regular "rite of passage".

From the first ride in a baby seat on the back of your parent's bike it never gets boring with 30 miles of bike trails. Then comes the summer of riding your own bike around and around the circle. Finally between the ages of 10 and 12 you and your cousins can go off to the mall alone – no parents. Oh! The joy of going to Goody's to spend the money you have been saving all winter and picking out your pieces of candy one by one with the wonderfully patient clerks. Then on to the Paper Station to buy stickers and such. These first excursions are very closely monitored by a mother or father who has sneaked down to the mall ahead of time to keep and eye on the little people.

It was a milestone the summer they all came and Grandad had built a wood play set. It had swings, a slide, ropes for climbing and a tree house. This was in great demand until the youngest grands reached ten or so, and it fell into disuse. Grandad dismantled it and gave it to a Habitat for Humanity family with four children.

Every evening after dinner we would have great games of soccer or volleyball until dark. Tennis was always a challenge. Both adults and children spent many happy hours in deep competition, summer after summer. Golf was an on-going sport for the adults and the two oldest boys who spent hours taking lessons and playing. Lest I forget the greatest excitement - when you were old enough to drive the golf cart around the circle. No one ever tired of going around until the batteries gave out, and the poor cart had to be pushed back to the garage for a recharge.

Grandad was always the one who decided when you were ready to hike. Not all the grandchildren made the cut, and some quit after the first ten mile hike, but all were eager to try. There were many, many picnics and fishing expeditions, and everyone enjoyed the fish.

Early on, Grandad bought a 17 foot boat, and learning to water-ski was the big challenge. Each summer at least one or two grands finally managed to get up and stay up. Many happy days were spent at Lake Billy Chinook skiing and picnicking.

The winter was an altogether different sport - skiing. When you reached the age of four, boys and girls alike, it was Mt. Bachelor and ski school. All the parents were avid skiers as was Grandad who took up downhill skiing at age 68. Grammie had sense enough to quit before her knees gave out.

When you have as large a group as we have, there are always card games, Monopoly, etc. in progress. The older boys kept their Monopoly game hidden in the attic - along with their favorite cereals to keep young fingers out.

What wonderful memories are built at Grammie and Grandad's house. If only all grandchildren could have such a magic place as Sunriver to do their growing.

SUNRIVER'S AMPHITHEATER

By
Robert C. Antle

Amphitheater! Sunriver has an amphitheater. I don't believe it!

Now this landmark is not one of the feature attractions that is pointed out to a guest by a proud Sunriver resident, and I doubt if any realtor ever has shown a prospective buyer this monument to our past. Yet, this structure is an integral part of Sunriver's history and topography. Where is it?

This imposing structure is on the left side of Beaver drive, less than a half-mile north of the mall encircled by lodgepole and ponderosa pine. From a distance, it could be a stadium where a Boy Scout waits to take you to your hard and backless seat, but there is no tunnel entrance. Or it could be a Roman arena built with slabs of stone by slaves to the glory of Caesar, but this edifice is of earth.

It stands in a semicircle with its back to our approach, an earthen mass approximately thirty feet high and about two hundred feet in length. A three foot high wooden railing surrounds the external periphery, as if to protect it. The pitch on this side is precipitous, a challenge to climb, but doable. Standing upon the ridge, the true amphitheater nature of the earth mass is apparent. On this inner side the slope is gradual, although in varying degrees. There are no seats. The view is disappointing, obstructed by trees, although to the north about two hundred yards is another dirt hill of similar height.

Unlike Stonehenge, there is no mysterious religious meaning to these promontories, nor is their history clouded. These masses were built by modern man about 1969. When the army abandoned Camp Abbott, the structures, barracks, hospital, fortifications were removed but the foundations were left. The developers of Sunriver found these piles of concrete and other artifacts a detriment to the development of the resort. Hide them! Yes these two huge mounds of earth are cover-ups. Everything unsightly, concrete, glass, rocks, metal, etc. were hauled to this area and covered with dirt.

John Gray, one of the founders of Sunriver, a true visionary, envisioned a sledding hill (the more northern mass) and an amphitheater with stone, immovable seats that would withstand the weather and vandals. (Vandals in Sunriver? Really!) The stage was to be of grass. Whether Gray imagined a well endowed soprano blasting an aria into the high desert atmosphere or whether he planned to stage a tragedy based on some Indian folklore like the "Trail of Tears", we shall never know.

Gray's dream was never finished. But could he have imagined the activity in his amphitheater when winters' white coat covers Sunriver. The children come in droves, some alone but many with dad and granddad. They pull their sleds, saucers, plastic strips and innertubes, and even garbage can tops (that will never fit again, but who cares.) The snow is deep, sledding is great and it's free. Cars sometimes clog Beaver drive, but our police do not play Scrooge and spoil the fun.

Exhausted, a happy boy, red cheeked with frosted eyebrows, and boots unlaced hangs on to granddad's hand. As the boy trudges in the deep snow he looks up and his eyes emit that glow of affection, that love, that his grandfather cherishes.

Yes, Sunriver does have an amphitheater.

BE C O C!
(Central Oregon Correct)

By
Dave Ghormley

People really watch what they are saying in Washington, DC, to be sure that they are "Politically Correct". If they didn't conform, they might lose their place on "THE network"- a fate worse than death itself.

Those of us who live in Central Oregon don't exactly care what's "PC" in Washington In fact, we've been known to go the other way and give "thumbs-down" to what the "beautiful people" think we should think.

As a public service, however we'd like to spend a moment or two orienting you on what's COC. You may find that you have to change your vocabulary and your way of doing things a tad if you want to get along with the rest of us.

Let us give you a few examples.

First off, be nice to "domers". Domers are tourists who have just picked up their condo keys and a map from the property manager, have bravely struck out for their vacation dream home on a dark, snowy night, have started around the second circle on the road, and ... are lost. They have pulled over to the side of the road with their maps out and their car's dome light on. Typically, there is a war going on in the car as the husband and wife argue over where they are and how they got there and the kids are screaming about needing a bathroom. You should approach with caution. The troops within may not be friendly. To be COC, you <u>will</u> try to help them out. You may make a friend for life, and you may find that this "tourist" is a super person. We've found that it pays to be helpful. That's COC.

It is recommended that you leave your jet at home. If that's too big a jolt to your life style, land at night, wear ragged old blue jeans when you arrive, and sneak over to the parking lot and get into the oldest, most beat-up pickup you can find to drive to your house. Jets are *not* COC.

When someone does something on the highway or on one of our streets that annoys you, such as going less than 70 or not pulling over onto the shoulder to let you pass when you lean on the horn, give the offender a friendly wave. Don't use one of those LA salutes where you only need one finger. Remember, most of us have a loaded shotgun in the cab of our pickup. We've been known to react strangely when we get hassled by a stranger.

If you own a recreation home at Sunriver, please remember that you're dealing with older folks in your daily elbow-rubbing with us "permanents". When you open up the house you haven't been in for months and go sashaying across the street to that wonderful neighbor you were so close to last summer to borrow a cup of sugar, don't feel bad if you get a blank look instead of an effusive greeting. We have a disease that is going around over here that we call Halfzimers or "Senior Moment Syndrome". They tell us it's normal and not to get agitated. We really do remember you and are glad you're back with us. It's just that we can't remember your name.

Now, as to language, here are some tips:

"World Class" is out. That's a phrase that Ted Turner's folks dreamed up to promote his "International News Service".

Forget "Have a Nice Day". That's an expression which got it's start with some switchboard gal in an LA advertising agency, and anything to do with LA and Advertising is suspect. Better just to skip "Have a Nice Whatever."

"Professional" is frowned on. A lot of us think this is your way of saying you're better than we are if you say you're a "professional" anything. Better leave this word for the wrestlers and the hookers.

When someone says to you something is a little "spendy", it means that the price of something whose price you haven't paid any attention to the whole time you were in "DC" or New York or LA is too high-priced in Central Oregon.

We call people who are in police work or fire suppression or postal delivery "policemen" or "firemen" or "postmen". It's just that we can't keep up with the latest Politically Correct lingo. We're trying, but bear with us.

When you go out to a party at Sunriver, if you insist on wearing that mink coat you found so alluring at some New York event a few weeks ago, be sure that everyone understands that it is "roadkill." You never know who is an Animalist.

It's OK for your kids to use words like "awesome" and "cool" and "out of sight", but you should forget words and phrases like "I'm focused on getting a job" and "I'm going to revisit the problem" and "women are a minority". These kinds of phrases are guaranteed to stir up problems for you.

Finally, when someone at a Sunriver party asks you where you are from and the answer is "California", respond, "Oh, just South of La Pine". It might save a "relationship", which, by the way, is another "no-no."

You're welcome in Sunriver- even if you're a "domer". However, the warmth of our welcome in is direct proportion to your desire to be COC- Central Oregon Correct.

45

FIREMAN SAVE MY CHILD

By
Robert C. Antle

Penthall, Young, Huetle, Britten, Haines, Cronen, Warren, Arnold, Carper, Ward, Lynch, Kappel, and the Weather brothers are names all Sunriver residents should remember. They were the first Sunriver firemen, all volunteers. Several, including Junior Kappel, who became their chief, had been volunteer fireman for the Salishan resort.

John Gray had developed the Salishan resort and in 1968, Gray opened Sunriver. It was natural that many employees migrated from Salishan to Sunriver. Most of the volunteer firemen were operational employees for the Sunriver resort. Kappel was superintendent of construction and maintenance when he assumed the post of fire chief—without a pay increase.

In October of 1968, Sunriver obtained its initial firetruck—a 1968 Ford, Western States. This truck could pump 750 gallons per minute with a booster pump. Fortunately this truck was identical to the truck Kappel and some of the men had used in Salishan. Kappel could devote his time to teaching the raw recruits the intricacies of the equipment. Recruits among the homeowners were a necessity, and some beguiling methods were used. Bill Larson was persuaded by Kappel to volunteer with, "If you don't and your house catches on fire, well".

Training sessions were held three Mondays a month for two hours. Both the La Pine and Bend fire departments were very cooperative. Chiefs from these cities taught classes in the Basic Training manual and worked with the Sunriver volunteers in simulated fire exercises.

But it was not all work. A pool table, beers in the fridge and many stories filled the firehouse which led to a wonderful camaraderie.

The first fire to test these recruits occurred in Bud Gilmore's cabin. Bud, a volunteer himself, noticed smoke coming from his house. He jumped in his car and sped to the station. It so happened that the truck was leaving the barn just when Gilmore arrived. He could not believe his eyes: Two men were hanging on the back bars, but there was no driver, at least he did not see the two men on the front seat. Running and screaming, "Fireman save my cabin", he chased the driverless truck.

One New Year's Eve a Meadow house belched smoke and the alarm sounded. A volunteer, Gene Vosbury arose tardily. He came running holding his pants knee high, finally reaching the firetruck. He sat on the tailgate to pull his pants up. Abruptly the truck took off leaving Vosbury flat on his 'keester'. Undeterred he took off running through the snowy woods, waving one hand while holding his britches with the other, but to no avail as he never caught the speeding truck.

Larson remembered a fire outside of Sunriver one wintry morning. It was three A. M. when they left the barn. Larson, hardly awake, hung from the back railing, as Kappel sped full-tilt, Andretti style, up Century drive. The highway was what every skier loathes, blue ice. Soon the firetruck was in a sideways schuss, back and forth, tailgate men stretched horizontal, while Kappel, terrified, struggled to keep that red devil upright and out of the ditch.

It was not long before a vehicle was obtained for medical emergencies. Funds from the Sunriver Woman's Club and Volunteer Fireman's association were used to update the vehicle and buy more advanced emergency trucks. Sunriver now owns an ambulance that carries a full compliment of basic and advanced life support equipment. Most of our active firemen have at least basic E M T training.

In September, 1972 Sunriver had a bomb scare. The fire department was advised that a bomb had been set to explode in the Sunriver lodge. This was an emergency. The fireman responded and attempted to evacuate the building. The lodge was brimming with patrons and they were not about to leave their turf and surf. Some patrons left the dining area to storm the bar. Others took their plates and stood outside, eating and observing. It was one evening checks were not paid.

In 1976 Steve Chandler was appointed as the first full time chief of the fire department. Five years later Sunriver fire department received a class 5 status over the previous class 7. This meant that the fire department was judged efficient and effective. This advanced status also substantially reduced insurance rates for owners.

The volunteers not only protected the residents but as early as 1969, they began the Fireman's Picnic, the Fireman's Ball and held potlucks in the firehall. About twice a year, the barn was cleared, tables set and the women prepared the goodies. Today the potlucks attract hundreds and are among Sunriver's most popular evenings.

The Fireman's Picnic is held every Fourth of July. It serves as a fund- raiser for the Firemen. In the early years the event was held at Mc Callum Park. One year the Eugene bag-pipers came to entertain. The music held up traffic on the Deschutes, as the people in the boats gathered, anchored and enjoyed the festivities.

The Fireman's Ball is held every Labor Day weekend. This is another fund-raiser with food, dancing and prizes. (This is one function that John Gray grandfathered. The

Great Hall is reserved for this event regardless of ownership of the hall.)

Today Sunriver has a modern fire station, modern equipment, and a excellent paid trained staff of about eight. A wonderful group of volunteers serve as back-ups. Emergency medical calls number about four hundred while about forty fires bring out the fire equipment annually. The Fire Department recently received a fire safety class 3 rating, further reducing the fire insurance rates.

Our fire protection has grown with the growth of Sunriver. We are fortunate to have the men and women who protect us today. But never should we forget the men who volunteered back in 1968 and the volunteers who followed, giving their time and risking their lives.

*My thanks to Junior Kappel. who supplied material for this article.

REVERSE LIVING

By

Frank Allen

The first houses I lived in had two or more windows at the front to give us more light in our living room. The dining room was behind the living room and the kitchen was at the back of the house. Bedrooms were on the same floor or could be upstairs. This general design was unchanged since the days of kerosene lamps.

When I first heard of "reverse living", builders described it as a house with the living room facing the back yard. The advantages were obvious. You or your guests could go directly from your picture windowed living room to your neatly landscaped back yard and enjoy the weather, your lawn, or your pool. You didn't have to look out and see the neighbor's cars parked on the street. Passers-by couldn't peek in your living room window and watch you or your guests. The kitchen frequently had a window on the street so the housewife could keep track of the kids in front or see visitors coming up the walk.

Originally the preponderance of Sunriver houses were modest second homes, ski cabins or summer retreats. But, as years passed, permanent residents, retirees and second home owners decided they wanted more space to accommodate visiting friends and their kids and grand-kids. The expanding Oregon economy and California retirees flush from selling their homes with huge capital gains provided more where-withal to build nicer and larger homes.

Architects have complained that smaller lots with the setbacks required by county regulations almost force a large house to have two stories. Is that bad? Many of these houses have the active living areas upstairs. Some bright and innovative architect or real estate agent changed the definition of "Reverse Living." Now it means living room, dining room, kitchen and possibly a bedroom are on the second floor. All other rooms are on the ground floor.

There are advantages and disadvantages to this plan. Reverse living can provide a better view of the forest, golf course or mountains from any upper floor room. Because heat rises, bedrooms downstairs are cooler. Residents tend to be in better physical shape because they must go up and down stairs.

One disadvantage of most reverse living houses is the stairway to the front door. Many steps are unprotected from the elements and must be cleared of snow and ice so they are safe. Clearing the steps, in itself, can be hazardous to one's health. Residents can overcome this by entering through the garage and then climbing an inside stairway. It's the safe but not stylish way for guests to enter. Since the kitchen is upstairs, groceries and many other items still must be carried up-stairs unless a dumb waiter is available.

Most reverse living houses have expansive decks. Handrails around decks must be designed to OSHA standards to keep toddlers from falling and yet not be so restrictive that they block views. In the wintertime decks become covered with snow and may require clearing should we get four feet of snow like the winter of '93-94. Lower level rooms of these houses usually are darker than the upper rooms because the decks above block much of the light.

My preference is a single floor plan, or, if more bedrooms are needed, put them upstairs. Upside down houses are not my cup of tea.

THE VILLAGE THEORY WORKS!

By
Dave Ghormley

We hear a lot of talk these days about village life and its importance. This is old-hat in Sunriver. Sunriver was originally laid out with a "village" concept in mind. The early developers visualized a series of separate groupings of homes and condos, linked together by lousy streets. At one point the thought was that everyone would park at a central place and then get around Sunriver by golf cart or bicycle or roller skates or, perish the thought, on foot! Needless to say, we couch-potatoes wouldn't put up with this kind of thinking, but the flavor of the "village" concept still lingers.

If you read your deed carefully, you will find that your Sunriver property is in a "village". If you look at a plat map of Sunriver, you will find that it is platted as a series of "villages". Over the years the thought of making each village distinctive and self-contained disappeared, but we still have the vestiges of this grand plan with us.

Of course, everyone likes to feel that he is a part of a group; so some of us still think of ourselves as members of one village or another. In my case, I'm in River Village #1. Others are in Overlook Park, Meadow Village, Sky Park, Fairway Crest, etc.

I don't know if the village concept will ever be more than a name in Sunriver, but it does help segregate us from another group of Sunriverites. And, more importantly, it gives us a common anchor to swing from with our non-resident neighbors.

You see, only about 20% of the homes and condos in

Sunriver are occupied by "permanent" residents, and even that number is suspect because of a voracious appetite to travel and get out of the snow exhibited by everyone who votes here. That means that every neighborhood is full of empty houses and condos most of the time. Still, everyone wants to get to know "the neighbors" and stay tuned on issues which affect the neighborhood in which their home is located.

So, when you go to a cocktail party or a pot luck or a church social, one of the early questions you ask a stranger is, "where do you live?", and if the answer is that the person resides in your village, a bond is born.

Unfortunately, the size of the villages is considerably larger than a true "neighborhood"; so some of us have developed smaller groupings. For example, in our neighborhood we have combined three or four adjacent lanes into a formidable group known as "The River Rats" named in honor of our River Village status.

The River Rats meet quarterly, or so, at a neighbor's house. We have a potluck or a cocktail buffet. It's up to the host/hostess, but we try to bring in as many of the part-time residents as possible so that everyone has a chance to get acquainted. We've even built a work party or two around River-Rat-Gatherings and cleared brush in the commons, etc. We've all gotten a little better acquainted because of all this activity, and the inclusion of the part-timers who are at Sunriver on the date set for the get-together has added a whole new, great dimension to our parties.

One thing we have all found out from this cross-exposure is that our events are a lot more interesting because we all bring fresh stories to the group. I get pretty tired of the same old jokes and gossip of the "regulars". It's fun to hear how our occasional neighbors are getting along, what they are thinking and experiencing, what is the latest gossip in Portland or Eugene or Seattle or San Francisco or Los Angeles.

We have found that some of our closest friends come from the "part-timers". We look forward to their visits and build our social schedule with their itineraries in mind. At the same time, they enjoy being part of a Sunriver group. It gives them a chance to keep in touch, find out what's going on here, and feel more comfortable when they are here. They don't have to bring a car full of friends to insure themselves of a fun experience. It works.

Sunriver is a resort community. There are always vacant houses and condos, strangers, newcomers. Some, like me, found the community so alluring that we moved here full-time. But we came from a bigger community. We enjoy the input of fresh comment and, especially, new jokes. We don't get insular and close-minded. It isn't for everyone, but it works for those who live here.

I don't know what is behind all the "village" talk on TV these days, but maybe we are a microcosm which can attest to the fact that it's a plus.

THE DESIGN AND PLANNING OF SUNRIVER

By

Glen Bending

Early in 1978, Sunriver was conceived to be a magnificent place which would be worthy of every effort to direct its growth into the far future.

In order to preserve the natural beauty of the forest, river, and mountain environment it was considered to be essential to augment the forest as houses displaced many of the trees. The houses were to be surrounded by newly planted trees as well as by the cherished older trees which must be carefully preserved during the construction of the homes, roads, paved bicycle paths, golf courses, swimming pools, tennis courts, playgrounds, quaint shops, airport, observatory, restaurants, and lodge. It was appreciated that every house and structure have a sphere of influence and that this aura is directly related to their prominence and visual impacts.

A Design Review Committee was designated to recognize these spheres of influence and to firmly defend the integrity of the forest environment. Five or even ten or more of the Ponderosa Pines were to be planted as necessary to reestablish the forest. It was clearly understood that these trees are the strongest and most effective way to mitigate and soften the presence of a house or other structure.

Most groups and individuals within Sunriver wish to preserve the quality of life that exists here. However, understanding the nature of Sunriver may be deficient in the very young and in some of the new arrivals. Therefore, constant communication setting forth the goals of Sunriver and its past, must be stressed as an integral part of all future planning and development.

Sunriver will flourish but it needs guidance, understanding, and love.

Currently, 80% of the homes in Sunriver have spas and adjacent recreational amenities. Some of the owners have wanted to have complete privacy by installing fences on their property lines and they valued their isolation more than their respect for the environment. Strangely, this desire for personal privacy was usually accompanied by unwillingness to allow other homes to build the offending fences. Many bitter battles have been fought to save the beauty of the community.

The committee was recently involved in a dispute with a builder who wanted to fence his entire property, much to the chagrin of his neighbors. He initially applied to build an extensive fence around a trampoline and this was approved but only with a much reduced area of fencing. The builder then submitted a plan for a large swimming pool with the request for the original extensive fencing. After careful consideration the plan was approved with the stipulation that both fence and pool would be built concurrently. The builder objected because he wanted to build the fence immediately and the pool only at some undetermined future date.

The Design- Review committee has been very busy, and it has been dogged by both praise and criticism over the years of its efforts on behalf of Sunriver.

CIRCLES GO NOWHERE, OR DO THEY?

By
Robert C. Antle

Visitors to Sunriver are befuddled by our circles, yet these same circles are important directional landmarks. "How do I get to Winners Circle?" a lost visitor will ask. With all those other lanes to use, why did he pick a street with circle in it to explain my point? Bizarre!

"Go straight to Circle Eleven, first outlet right, then to Circle Ten, half way around, then to Circle Nine, first outlet, right, second intersection, turn left. You're there. Remember cars in the circle have the right-of-way." "Would you repeat that?"

Circles are magical. I can remember Mr. Purdy, the writing instructor, who came to our second grade class. "Use your arms, that flowing motion." His demonstration, beautiful symmetrical circles, one after another were spellbinding. Discouraged with my efforts, he remarked, "You should be a doctor".

The developers knew what they were doing when Sunriver was laid out with circles instead of stop-lights. Phew, pollution with every stop, worse when the power is out. Keep the high desert air clean.

Planet Earth orbits in almost a circle. It is much more fun to travel somewhere and back in a circle, rather than retracing one's steps. Probably the greatest invention of all was the wheel. Can you imagine life sans wheel? Just try driving on a flat tire!

Practically every game depends upon a circle. From the ball in jacks to soccer, basketball, volleyball, billiards, tennis, to name a few, depend upon that wonderful circle.

57

Badminton and football are anomalies. Upsets in football are the result of those crazy bounces. The ball isn't round.

Have you ever seen a halo that wasn't round? And what about the vicious circle? It goes round and round like those rides at the fair. It is enough to upset one's stomach. And if it were not for a circle, who would have ever heard of "Pi", or diameter and circumference?

You see, I am enamored of circles and a proponent of Sunriver circles even if number eight is missing in Sunriver. Circles instead of red and green lights are common in European countries. What an advantage, when one errs, to just keep going round and round until one can make the proper exit. Circles are a splendid location to honor local heroes. I often keep circling so I can read the inscription on a statue. Also the center of the circle lends itself to lovely displays of flowers~another reason to take an additional lap.

P.S. Trying to put a golf ball in that circular hole can be as frustrating as driving in Sunriver.

JOE'S MAP

By
Frank Allen

It was dusk and Joe and Ann were lost! They were looking for the home of their friends Peter and Joyce who had moved to Sunriver just a year ago. Joe slowed as he entered Sunriver and turned right between a gas station and a market. "What's their address? Wasn't it some evergreen?" Joe asked. Ann reached into her purse. "Here it is!....14 Pine Needle Lane." Then Ann looked for the map they had received from Peter while Joe continued looking for a spot to pull off the road. There weren't any wide spots but he found a cleared area and pulled over.

As Joe unfolded the map he realized he needed the dome light to decipher all the wiggly streets and lanes. He reached for a tissue to wipe his reading glasses. Why are names on all maps in such fine print? He reasoned, if Sunriver was like most 20th Century towns, the street names would be organized somehow. Some towns have only numbered and lettered streets. Others have streets named for alphabetically listed trees or presidents. For example, if you know your history and presidents in Corvallis, you can figure in which direction to go to your destination. In some towns the streets are perpendicular to avenues. But when a town has grown and has more than 26 streets or avenues, the rest of them are seldom organized.

Joe knew that Sunriver was a planned community and should be organized, Pine Needle Lane should be near other trees. He studied the map in the dim light and found Poplar and Red Cedar and Hickory and Fircone but no Pine

Needle. Then he found Raccoon, Grizzly and Bobcat and realized this was the zoo section. He looked further and found Hart Mountain, Mt. Adams and Mt. St. Helens. All mountains, but no trees! Then he found Tournament Lane, Winners Circle and Trophy Lane. Now there was organization: enter the Tournament, get in Winner's Circle and take the Trophy. Why didn't they do more of that.

Sunriver is a village of trees, mountains, animals, golf terms and circles, all of which are not organized, although some are loosely grouped. But are the groups organized? Is Lodgepole near Poplar or Ponderosa near Cedar. Is Maury Mountain Lane near Crater or Lava Top? No! Joe began to realize there must be an easier way to find Pine Needle Lane. Then he found the index at the top of the map.

Suddenly a red light shone through the back window and shortly a police officer was at his window. "Sir, There is no roadside parking here in Sunriver, but, tell me where you want to go and I believe I can get you on you way." The officer showed Joe where he was, and then quickly marked the map to show the route to Pine Needle. He said, "Sunriver, with its circles and curving roads, is a confusing place to drive, especially for the first few times. We have many people stop to look at a map with their dome light on. Our narrow roads don't have shoulders and we would prefer that visitors stop in the village parking lot to look at the map before they proceed. We've recently installed a kiosk near each entrance with large maps to help visitors find their way. Have a nice visit." And he was gone.

Joe was relieved. No ticket, so his car insurance premium wouldn't go up. He and Ann followed the marked map and, except for missing a turnoff at one of the circles, and going around twice, soon arrived at Peter and Joyce's pride and joy.

60

FRIENDLY FRENZY

By
Dave Ghormley

Detroit should send their engineers to Sunriver before they finalize their newest car designs.

We pride ourselves on our friendliness. We smile at each other a lot, we wave and call out a good old Western "Howdy", we reach out to newcomers, we care!

However, some of the new features in car design are creating problems.

You see, when you drive on Sunriver's picturesque but winding streets and lanes, you should be paying attention. Pine trees come right up to the edge of the roads and squirrels or deer have a habit of darting out in front of you unexpectedly. If you haven't got your wits about you, you can end up with a tree in your front seat or conducting a squirrel's funeral, neither of which is recommended.

At the same time, in the spirit of friendliness, it's nice to wave hello to a friend approaching you as you drive along. However, since we are a reserved and proper bunch, we need to be sure at whom we are waving in order to gauge the warmth and vigor of our greeting.

Here is where the car designers are failing us.

First, you can now buy cars with seats at various elevations from the street. So, you're either craning up or squinting down at the occupant of the approaching vehicle.

Secondly, instead of having six or eight feet of hood in front of the driver, there are more and more cars/trucks/vans/suv's with shorter and shorter distances between the front bumper and the driver. You must react much more quickly. Brain power must be working at top speed to relay

61

to you that this is a stranger or your best friend, and your waving and smiling muscles must react like lightning.

Thirdly, all cars look more and more alike. All the sports utility vehicles look alike at first glance. All the little Japanese sedans look alike. All the pickup trucks look alike. All the vans look alike. All the sports cars look alike. It used to be that you knew that one of your friends had a green Buick, another a gray Chevy- and the difference was obvious. No longer.

Finally, the windows on the cars are getting darker and darker so that it is harder and harder to see inside an approaching car.

This is very difficult. There just isn't time to concentrate on who is in that approaching car while watching for deer, trees, and the approaching circle at the same time. Since we are basically a friendly tribe and don't want anyone getting the idea that we're snobs or don't care, we are having a problem trying to stay alive getting from home to the post office. And since a lot of us are a little bit gray and wrinkly, we find ourselves driving like we have blinders on, not daring to glance at the oncoming driver. We know our brains just don't work fast enough any more to process the info and wave in time to do any good.

But we do care!

So what's the solution? That's why we need to get the auto designers to Sunriver to spend time with us. They must work out an answer before we all kill ourselves by being friendly or being ostracized by seeming unfriendliness.

My solution is very simple. It's like the "caller ID" system on the phone. Cars will come equipped with a sensor beam that sends out the driver's call letters. In addition, there will be an incoming receiver sensor that we can program so that when a friend is approaching, a buzzer will sound.

If the buzzer sounds, we will have time to screw on a smile and wave frantically. No buzzer, no wave. Just a slight nod. What could be simpler?

An optional extra would be a receiver that would give a Bronx cheer for someone you're mad at, allowing plenty of time for you to put your nose up in the air.

And with the new system in place the squirrels and deer and trees and traffic circles will be very appreciative, to say the least. The only loser I can think of would be Mike's Car Repair. Maybe we can get him the franchise for the sensors. If not, he'll just have to go out of the body-repair business and go back to putting stud tires on and off!

With the sensor system in place, we could stay friendly on the highway with a whole lot less frenzy and chaos.

Come on, Detroit and Yokohama. We need help!

* * * * * *

FISHING IN SUNRIVER

By
Keith S. Pennington

There once was a fisherman from Goose Bay

Whose catches were small, so they say

But while fishing the Deschutes

He hooked a tree by the roots

His Ponderosa was "The catch of the day"!!

SUNRIVER ANGLERS

By

Rex Henton

In the beginnings of Sunriver a group of early residents
became acutely aware of the pristine volcanic lakes and
streams which would enhance their living and recreating in
the high desert region of Oregon. Hence the founding of the
Sunriver Anglers twenty years or more ago. There were
eleven charter members.

During its early development the Anglers decided that
everyone did not fully appreciate fly fishing and the effective
utilization of fly rods. The primary goal of the club became
the art of tying flies which would produce the catch, and the
beginnings of hook and release of the Browns, Rainbows and
Brookies that thrive in the cool waters.

Over the years the club was mainly a male dominant
organization, but it was soon realized that there were women
who liked to fish as well. The membership was opened to all.

Monthly outings are a part of the Anglers program
during the fishing season. An area (lake or stream) is
selected, and team sponsors handle the waterside luncheon.
On occasion these have been gourmet presentations to satisfy
the taste buds and palates of all partakers. Most importantly,
however, has been the streamside meetings at lunch to
discuss the types of flies and lines which have helped in
luring the "wileys".

During the winter months various fly shops have been
available to teach fly tying and casting techniques. The fly
shops have produced their favorite flies for our high desert
region which have presented the most rewarding results.
Wooly buggers in all colors and elk hair caddiz have been

outstanding performers, depending on conditions and time of day.

Over the past twenty years the Anglers have worked in close coordination with the Oregon Department of Fish and Wildlife, the U. S. Forest Service and S.T.E.P. (Salmon and Trout Enhancement Program). The Angler volunteers have been involved in the S.T.E.P. program since its inception six years ago. This program involves over 500 school children from the Bend-LaPine school district as well as students from Tumalo and Redmond. The program concentrates on hatchery operations and fish spawning at stream side.

Each year the ODF&W counts Redds (spawning beds) in the rivers flowing into the lakes and reservoirs. The Anglers have tended the hatch boxes in Spring River and assisted in the releasing of 50,000 brown trout fingerlings each year for the past six seasons.

The Anglers have adopted the Fall River Hatchery as their special project. The hatchery is one of the oldest in Oregon, and its closure was planned, but our volunteers stepped in. It took two summers to paint the buildings and assist in grounds maintenance to insure its continued operation. We built a kiosk and assisted in the construction of a handicap rest room facility with heat and running water. With our assistance a renewed program for the hatchery and its importance to the region were realized.

A handicap ramp was constructed at Brown's River Crossing near the Crane Prairie Campground. This was a major building project conducted with the U.S. Forest Service and assisted by the Anglers.

For the past five years the Anglers have been involved in 'National Kids Fish Day" which has been held at the Sunriver Homeowners Mary McCallum Park. Fish from the Fall River Hatchery are released at the inlet eddy next to the Trout

House. Anglers, assisted by Forest Service personnel help children fish and conduct classes on the life cycle of fish. The day is culminated by the Anglers' service of "tube steaks" (hot dogs) to the grandparents, parents and all the happy anglers. Many times it is the first fishing experience for these children.

The next anticipated involvement of the Anglers is to assist the ODF&W and the U.S. Forest Service in implementing the Wild and Scenic River Project which borders over six miles of winding Sunriver river frontage. The ODF&W will use helicopters to place trees with roots and branches along the river banks on the Sunriver side. Rocks and trees will be placed in areas ideal for fish spawning as well as an attempt to stop river bank erosion. The Anglers will assist in the planting of willows on the banks where erosion will occur. This will be an expensive project but is essential to preserve our beautiful Deschutes River as a wild spawning ground for trout and especially the German Browns that are prolific in these waters.

The direction of Sunriver Anglers has been and will continue to be oriented toward volunteer involvement in improving the quality of living in Sunriver and protecting our pristine lakes and waters. We are dedicated to this premise and will take every opportunity to work to improve fish habitat wherever possible. Dynamic community relations are at the forefront of our club's mission statement and will continue with the same dedication in the future.

On behalf of Sunriver Anglers, "May your lines be tight, your reels singing, and the wind to your back!"

SPRING IN SUNRIVER

By
Keith S Pennington

The Deschutes river full and flowing swiftly by
Ponderosa swaying to the music of the wind
Snow capped mountains reaching to the sky
As the cool earth 'wakens to Spring
The airport windsock fluttering to and fro
Planes landing before the wind
The warmth of a sun, that now rides high
As Sunriver greets the new Spring

Swallows finding their way back, as winter leaves
Songbirds merrily frolicking on wing
Geese trumpeting loudly from an unbalanced V
Each, perfoming their ode to Spring
Children playing in Fort Rock park
Running joyfully 'twixt slide and swing
Their voices ringing high, like that of a lark
Singing out to greet the new Spring.

The full moon gazing from a cirrus sky
Moonstruck shadows dancing to the wind
The flutter of night birds seeking their prey
Midst the last snow flakes of Spring
Deer returning to graze in the woods
Aspen leaves learning to quake with the wind
Tulips and daffodils follow the suns rays
Bringing new life to all living things

The Lodge sillouetted against a deep blue sky
Golfers endlessly practicing their swing
From tee to green as the white balls fly
Nature harkens to the coming of Spring
The Mall casting off it's winter coat,
Now dons tables and chairs for relaxing
People casually dine 'neath the noonday sun
While nature continues her "Springing"

As Sunriver welcomes this coming of Spring
T'is now my hope above 'most everything
That the Giver of Life and Lord of all Things
Lets me witness Sunriver greet many more Springs.

JOHN HOLM

68

A GARDENER'S PARADISE

By

Dave Ghormley

If you love flowers and plants and lots of home-grown fresh vegetables, forget living in Sunriver- unless, of course, you enjoy pain. However, if you are willing to fight back, the payoff can be great.

To begin with, outdoor gardening here is a four month endeavor, maximum. The ground is frozen hard as a rock until mid March. When you are about ready to jump off the roof and end it all, a crocus sticks its head up out of the ground. The next day, a few more emerge, to be followed in short order by all manner of small bulbs and daffodils and dwarf iris and tulips and narcissi. You have no idea how good those little pinpoints of color in the drab, cold, brown garden make you feel. Everything hasn't died and passed away! There is hope!

However, you have many other lessons to learn. For example, you find out that deer think of tulips the way that you think of ice cream. It is hard to describe the feeling you will get when you take some friends out to the garden on a chilly April evening to show them your beautiful new catalogue-bought tulips and find yourselves in the midst of a bevy of hungry does with your beautiful tulip blossoms hanging out of their mouths!

Well, shucks, you don't have to use the whole yard for flowers. You'll just plant some planters and put them on the deck and the deer won't bother. Lots of luck!

Next, you rush up to the nursery in town and load up on pansies and petunias and alyssum and marigolds and zinnias and impatiens and all manner of luscious delights. You start in early May so things can grow and give you a full summertime of beauty. You put some cloth covers over the planters because you know there is a remote possibility of a late freeze. But one night you forget.

One of two things happen. Either the freeze hits or the deer sneak up onto the deck and chew up every last blossom and plant. In either event, adios plants. It's back to the nursery for another load.

In the meantime, you have staked out the vegetable garden. You find interesting things there, too. First, vegetable plants freeze, too. Secondly, deer like vegetables. Thirdly, all manner of insects, mold, aphids and other assorted creepy, crawly things like vegetables. And finally, you find after a season or two of zealously fighting off all of the above that there is a guy in Bend with a great vegetable stand who can supply you with all of the vegetables you can eat at a fraction of the cost of homegrown. And he just hauled them over from some farm in the Willamette Valley, where they had been picked the day before.

The grass grows beautifully. All it takes is water and fertilizer. Don't pay any attention to the water bill or the fertilizer bill or the cost of the guy who cuts the grass once a week. Think positively. Doesn't that green grass just look great?

Of course, the cost does bother a little. It runs about twice what you've ever paid anywhere else for twelve months of grass, not just four months worth!

You decide to plant some specimen trees to relieve the monotony of jack pines. So you bring in some Scotch pines, some Austrian pines, some mountain ash, some birch and aspen trees. Ah! Now that's more like it.

You might get one year. That would be maximum. The porcupines will girdle the pine trees. The flickers will girdle the birch and the mountain ash. A wonderful fungus called "black leaf" will attack the aspen. And if you live near the river, that funny sound you will hear during the night will probably be the beaver hauling away those nifty, succulent young aspen and birch.

So, after a couple of years of all this you must make a few basic decisions.

First, why don't you forget the whole idea and let the native plants and trees grow up around you. Let the ponderosa and jack pines take over, let the bitter brush and the manzanita be the shrubbery. Buy a couple of pounds of wildflowers and plant some fescue grasses and throw a little water and fertilizer at them every couple of weeks. And go play golf or go fishing. That's option one.

Or if you must have a garden, ask someone who's been around what to plant that the deer won't eat. There isn't much, but there are possibilities.

Or, if you insist on raising deer food and aspen and birch and Scotch pine, find out where to buy fencing and trunk wrap and freezer cloth and deer repellent and deer whistles and motion detectors with sirens.

Then you can sit back and enjoy all of the glories of a Sunriver garden, but enjoy it quickly, because come October 1, it is going to disappear.

One day you will have tubs full of glorious flowers that you have jealously guarded and nurtured all summer long. The next day you will find a sea of drooping plants in a tub of snow. Winter's here! Throw them all away and light the fire and get out the bulb catalogues for next year. And keep telling yourself that it was worthwhile.

Spring's coming and hope springs eternal! Right?

THE AIRPORT AT SUNRIVER

By
Glen Bending

The Airport was built at the time of the initial planning and construction. The Army Corps of engineers had not been involved in any airport planning at Camp Abbot.

We are not sure why John Gray included the concept of a "fly in" resort development but we can be grateful that he was wise enough to foresee that it would have a profound effect on the future of Sunriver.

The airport is blessed with the plenitude of clear days of sunshine and safe flying for non-instrument rated pilots. This is in marked contrast to the frequently overcast and rainy weather in the Willamette valley just over the Cascade mountains to the west.

However, there is an instrument approach for the very rare times when the runway is "socked in." Since the airport is at an altitude of over 4,000 feet, the FAA conducts refresher programs on safe high altitude flying.

Many pilots have flown into Sunriver in their small to large private aircraft; fallen in love with the area; and built homes. Many of these are large mansions with attached hangars so that the pilots can taxi directly into these homes. There are very few situations comparable to this anywhere else in the world. Certainly, these pilots have been unusually intelligent and adventurous and they have greatly influenced the community.

Many national and international flying organizations have held their conventions and meetings at the resort here and these have ultimately contributed new residents. After all, where else can anyone find the fine airport, the skiing, the Trout fishing, the golf, tennis, white water rafting and the amenities of a world class resort.

Sunriver has the busiest private airport in Oregon and, at times, hundreds of aircraft are parked and these range from small to larger multi engine jets.

The airport has definitely added a flair and a dimension which has been very valuable. Many interesting people have moved to Sunriver from distant parts of the country and from around the world, in part, due to the flying facilities.

ONLY A STONE'S THROW AWAY

By
R. C. Antle

"I guess we're matched together, I'm Sam Square from Sedra Woolly, Washington."

"I'm Duke Dixon from here in Sunriver. I'm having a quick coffee and roll. Care to join me?"

"Great idea"

Sitting outside the golf shop, they sipped their java and munched their rolls. It was just past seven A.M., a beautiful central Oregon morning.

"So you live right here in Sunriver. Retired? It's my first visit to Sunriver. Looks like quite a spot."

"I love it. Retired five years ago from Salem. You on vacation? Any children?"

"My annual week with the kids. Molly, my wife, is getting some groceries and renting bikes for the youngsters. I figured this was my only chance to golf. They'll be waiting, raring to go. So much to do, don't know where to start."

"Sam, although Sunriver offers a lot, don't miss the many fun areas just a stone's throw away. How old are the children?"

"Ten and twelve."

"Perfect. Sam, hope you don't think it's presumptuous, but I think I can help, at least it works for our grandchildren. I use the half day scheme, half in, half out.

"Today for instance, pack a lunch, then head back 97 a few miles. On your left you'll see Lava Lands. Take the gravel road four miles to Benham falls. Wonderful spot for a picnic. Then walk about half a mile along the Deschutes, placid at first, then a roar of plunging water. A true cataract, quite spectacular. After that thrill, drive back to the visitor's center. Here you'll learn all about the area from every aspect. Take a couple of trails, one goes right up on the lava. A bus to the top of the butte will complete your day.

"After supper, take a bike ride.

"One day, take in Paulina peak area Drive to the top. The vista is comparable to Crater lake. View the obsidian, take a short hike and lunch near the falls. Take some Off. Mosquitoes can ruin your picnic.

"Another day take in the Lava Caves. Then go to the High Desert Museum. Plan about three hours. Not only is the museum wonderful, but the animal exhibits are terrific. The kids will love the otters, Ernie and Bert. Don't miss the Desert Museum.

"Do the children like to hike, Sam?"

"Oh, sure, they think it's a blast."

"Take off early and drive up Century drive to the Green lakes trailhead. Pack a lunch and hike along Fall creek up to the most beautiful lakes, bluish green. I think it's the best hike in the area. Then take the kids to Elk lake. Good spot to cool the feet. Be sure to go in the restaurant and order some milk-shakes. Wonderful, especially the marionberry. On your return, stop at Bachelor and take the lift to the summit. Tremendous views. Then take the family to one of the Sunriver pools. Now that is a complete day."

"It Sounds great," said Sam.

Duke continued. "Kids like to fish?"

"They sure do."

"One evening take the family to the Trout House for dinner. Be sure the children have their fishing gear. They'll finish dinner first so they can go outside and drop a couple lines. You can observe from the window. Often children land a few trout right off the dock. Maybe you'll have fish for breakfast.

"Sam, I hope this gives you an idea of how to explore and enjoy central Oregon."

"That's quite an agenda, Duke. We'll give it a try, thanks. Hey, wasn't that our names? We're on the tee."

PUBLISHER

By
Annis Oetinger

I once knew a Sunriver writer.

He wrote texts both heavy and lighter.

All he had on his mind

Was a publisher to find.

If his writing were better, he might-a!

CALL OF THE WILDLIFE

By

Mel Johnson

The sign on the little railroad station platform read "Chemult", and Calvin knew that his tedious train trip was over. In little more than a day he had witnessed changes from the brown land, air and people of southern California to the blue sky, green trees, and white, snow-capped mountains of central Oregon.

The eleven-year-old boy was relieved to see his grandparents, Clara and Bob, standing by to greet him as he stepped down from the train. After a bear hug from Clara and a man-to-man handshake from Bob, they were quickly on their way to Sunriver, his grandparents' home.

As they traveled north, Calvin listened with pleasure when Bob described the many summer activities available to a young fellow his age, and Clara guaranteed him an ample supply of her famous chocolate cake and homemade ice cream. From their description, Calvin anticipated a fun-filled vacation in a woodland paradise.

When they turned off the highway toward the entrance to Sunriver, Bob remarked, "Remind me to stop at the checking-in station to have you dipped."

Startled, Calvin asked, "Dipped? What for?"

"Ticks," Bob replied. "You may not know it, but all people coming in from southern California must be dipped at the Sunriver border. It's the law. Sunriver is very protective of its wildlife, and I could be sent to jail for allowing someone to cross the line without being dipped if they brought in the dreaded Squirrel Fever."

"I don't have any ticks," protested Calvin. "What if you

just didn't tell anyone that I came from California?"

They both looked at Clara who shrugged. "I suppose we could do that," she said. "But you would have to be earmarked."

"That's right," Bob nodded. "We would have to notch one of your ears to show that you haven't been dipped just in case a plague broke out, wiping out the squirrel herds. Then the Rangers could easily spot the one who brought the disease into Sunriver, and they would know who to hang."

Calvin thought for a minute, and then said, "All right, I might as well get it over with and be dipped."

He looked at Clara who was covering her mouth with one hand. He saw her eyes were sparkling as though she were trying to keep from laughing. The corners of Bob's mouth were turning up, and he seemed to be holding his breath.

Calvin suddenly realized that he had just been made the victim of a hoax, like some yokel being taken by a couple of city slickers. The laugh was on him. Blushing, he agreed, feeling like someone who had just fallen off the turnip truck. He vowed to himself not to be taken in so easily next time.

They were chuckling when they turned in to Sunriver. Bob pointed out some of the major spots of interest starting with the shopping mall. They visited the Great Hall, the Nature Center, the mighty Deschutes River and Fort Rock Park on the way to their house overlooking the Woodlands Golf Course.

Calvin was shown to his room. While he unpacked, Bob started grilling hamburgers on the deck while Clara brought out large bowls of chili beans, potato salad, and a chilled watermelon. Calvin noted how quiet it was here in the forest compared to the tumult of his home in the city. Only the sound of the wind in the trees and the honking of a flock of geese overhead broke the silence.

Beginning to relax, he was reaching for a slice of watermelon when a long, blood-chilling howl was carried in on the breeze. It was a sound that thousands of years before had caused Stone Age men to reach for their spears and throw another log on the fire. Later, mountain men would put out their fires and look to their powder in case the cry came from an Indian instead of an animal.

"What was that?" Calvin asked, staring wide-eyed into the forest. Bob didn't even look up from his dinner.

"Coyote," he answered. "Sounds like a big one."

"Are they dangerous?" Calvin inquired.

"Only if you get them riled up," replied Bob. "Although we believe they might have taken a friend of mine a few years ago. It was about this time of year when old Roy vanished. He was quite a character - spent most of his time on the golf course. Played left-handed. Chewed tobacco around the clock. Used to spit tobacco juice in the cup every time he three-putted a green. Nobody liked to follow his foursome. Then one night he just disappeared. They found his golf shoes at the foot of his bed, and a plug of Mail Pouch under his pillow, but they never found hide nor hair of Roy. We think the coyotes got him. Took him out through an open window. We searched the woods for several days. Finally hired a tracker, but all he found were the buttons of Roy's pajamas up in the rimrocks. Golf just hasn't been the same around here since we lost old Roy."

As if to support Bob's tale, another mournful howl floated out of the forest wilderness. This one seemed to be a little closer. Calvin's only perception of these animals came from Hollywood productions where great, hairy, red-eyed creatures with dripping fangs menaced gentle forest denizens and fleeing trappers.

"Now, Bob, don't be scaring the boy with your wild yarns," Clara said as she gathered up the dishes. "We'd better go in, it's getting dark."

Obediently they followed her into the kitchen. After the dishes were done, Calvin announced that it had been a long day, and he was ready for bed.

Bob and Clara retired about an hour later, and the house grew dark and silent. Although he was very tired, Calvin was still lying awake. Tossing and turning, he couldn't rid his mind of the notion that Bob could make the most outrageous story seem believable. On the other hand, those alarming howls from the wilderness had come from real animals. Probably animals with sharp teeth and claws.

Finally he couldn't stand it any longer. He got up, crossed the room, and quietly closed the window.

MARCH GOLF

By
Frank Allen

The morning sun is doing its best to shine brightly in between some gathering gray storm clouds. Behind us, half the sky is azure blue. Pat Whelan's weather report said the sky would be blue overhead, but he also told us we will have scattered clouds and possible showers in a breezy afternoon.

Jack is the perfect picture of a cross country skier who was challenged at the last moment to play a round of golf. The man is relatively warm because his long johns, a turtle neck tee shirt, a wool ski sweater and a windbreaker keep his torso warm. His legs are protected by his long handles, under shorts and a pair of wool slacks. But his legs are not warm! The frigid breeze seems to blow right through them. But Jack is a long time golfer and golfers are prepared. He pulls his rain pants from the jacket pocket of his golf bag and slips them on. Finally, his legs are warm. A billed golf cap doesn't keep you warm, so Jack wears a wool ski hat over the summer golf cap. A thin leather golfer's glove covers his left hand, but on his right he has a nylon sports glove with vinyl spots to allow it to get a good grip.

Jack pulls a wooden tee from his jacket pocket. Five more tees and two ball markers fall on the turf as his gloved hand pulls the pocket inside out. He turns, mutters an obscenity, gathers up the errant items and puts them back in his pocket with and ungloved hand. He positions a tee under an experienced white ball and attempts to press it into the grayish green turf. The ground under the grass is hard, or to be honest, it is frozen. A harder push and it is set. A gust of wind blows the Maxfli off its prop. After remounting the ball, Jack feels under his jacket sleeve with one hand to grasp the end of his polypropylene long johns. He must get rid of a bothersome wrinkle at his elbow before he can properly address the ball.

White flakes from an oncoming dark squall line bite Jack's smooth shaven cheek as he sets up for his first shot. He wonders if he would be warmer with a beard. He has already gone through a series of twisting gyrations and light calisthenics to make sure he is not stiff in the cold breeze. To fight this strong wind, Jack selects his driver to keep the ball low.

A three wood might be used on a normal day. Toe tips are aligned parallel to the anticipated flight of the missile. Knees are slightly bent. His grip has been practiced over and over and feels perfect. He takes a practice swing and everything seems ready. After addressing the ball, the long shafted Callaway driver is brought back in a smooth tempo. Then, like a pendulum in a hurry, the club swing reverses and arcs forward, hitting the ball with a definite high pitched tone, and follows through.

All eyes search the advancing cloud of snow for the fast departing speck. The ball makes a low flat trajectory and bounds forward off the frozen ground. Several long bounces seem to offset the braking effect of the wind, and Jack observes there are some benefits playing golf when it is so cold. With a shot like that, this could be a good day.

SOAP OPERA

By
Annis Oetinger

Once upon a time a group of middle-age men came to Sunriver. To be exact, they were a shade past middle-age, and there were twelve of them, three foursomes. The group had been getting together every year at different places for a golf tournament. This particular year it was to be at Sunriver.

The chairman for the year rented a nice house large enough to accommodate twelve. Each man was assigned a job on a rotating basis from year to year. Some were cooks, some were on KP and some planned the golf.

Part of the cooks took care of breakfasts, and part were responsible for dinners. These usually consisted of items not requiring exotic ingredients or a great degree of capability in the kitchen. One night the menu featured turkey breast with stove-top stuffing, and the other night it was ham with baked potatoes. As long as a person could read and follow directions on the package, either menu was reasonably fool-proof. Good, too.

Now, dear readers, this particular year which I'm telling you about, Harold and George were in charge of cleaning up after dinner the first night. While the rest of the group retired to the living room in well-fed comfort, these two headed for the kitchen. Leftovers were stashed in the refrigerator for subsequent snacks. Gradually our stalwart KP'ers worked their way through the dishes, loading them into the dishwasher in surprisingly neat fashion. A few pots and pans would have to be done by hand.

"Okay, now," Harold said, "we've got the thing all loaded. Where's the soap?"

"Right here," and George handed him a bottle of dishwashing stuff. Harold filled the little cups on the door of the dishwasher, shut it and turned the dial to start. He and George prepared to wash the pans while the dishwasher groaned and clicked into its appointed cycle.

The fearsome twosome were diligently scrubbing and wiping the pans and cleaning up around the place when George noticed some foam coming out around the edge of the dishwasher door.

"Hey, what's that?" he asked.

"What's what?" Harold replied.

"That foam there. Should it be doing that?" By now the foam was oozing out in considerable quantity and running down onto the floor.

"Well, how the hell should I know if it should be doing that?" Harold asked. "I don't know anything about dishwashers. Jenny won't let me touch ours. Says I don't do a good job. Anyway, I suppose they're all different."

"I don't know," George shook his head dubiously. "I don't think this is right." By now the foam was spreading out on the floor. "We better mop this up I think," and he took some towels in hand.

Allow me to digress a moment. Do you remember, dear readers, the story you might have read in third grade about the poor old couple who were often hungry? The good-wish fairy granted them a wish, and they wished for a pot on the stove that would never be empty. The good fairy gave them what they asked for. The pot produced a full meal of rice and produced more and more and more - so much that it ran all over the kitchen, filled their house and ran outside and down the road. They had neglected to find out how to turn it off.

This was the condition in which our two intrepid

cleaner-uppers found themselves. Soap suds boiled out of the dishwasher in a foaming mass spilling across the floor faster than they could mop. Frantically, they used towel after towel, and still the suds came in billowing clouds spreading toward the living room.

"This is terrible," George wailed. "The other guys are out there resting up for the golf tomorrow, and we're gonna be up all night cleaning this mess. We'll be exhausted. How can we play golf and win if we're worn out?"

"How do I know?" Harold rasped. "There oughta be something we can do to stop this thing. Why don't we just turn it off?"

"What's going on out there?" someone called from the living room.

"Uh, we got a little problem," Harold answered "Anyone know what's wrong with this dishwasher?"

"Good god, what'd you do?" one of the other golfers asked when he saw the suds.

"I don't know," Harold grumped. "Never saw anything like this before. Just trying to clean things up, and the damn machine went berserk."

"This what you put in?" the man asked. "No wonder. This is liquid soap for washing dishes in the sink. You should have used the dishwasher detergent."

"Well, now we turned the thing off, let's go to bed and finish up tomorrow."

"You'll have to get up early to get it all cleaned up before breakfast," the chairman said. "We don't have enough dishes for breakfast without what's in the dishwasher."

Ten men went to their rest snickering, and two went in weary disgruntlement.

Next morning saw the two cleaning up as best they could. The dishwasher insisted upon spewing out more suds

85

as it finished its cycle. At least the kitchen floor was sparkling clean. The weary workers threw the endless towels in the dryer and collapsed to await breakfast.

According to my informants, Harold and George were not the only culinarily-challenged in the group. I'm told someone put the soda pop in the freezer, and the baked potatoes exploded in the oven. It might seem that this group should not have been allowed out alone in the world without their mothers, or better yet, their wives. My informant did not tell me who won the golf tournament.

The group felt that perhaps they would not be too welcome at Sunriver the next year although they really enjoyed themselves mostly. They let a few years go by, giving their patronage to other unfortunate resorts from year to year. BUT - I'm told they were able to make a reservation here for this next year. Enough time had passed that the memory of their previous visit had faded. So everyone watch out. Who knows what this band will do? On the other hand, they're a few years older, quite definitely past middle-age. Perhaps they have slowed down a bit now, and - dare we hope - they've learned a thing or two.

SUMMER IN SUNRIVER

By
Keith S. Pennington

Ponderosa slowly stretch their shadows
As they greet a new Sunriver dawn
Casting fragrant vapors into the cool mountain breeze
While the sun rises to bring the new morn

Mists slowly rise above river and field
The dawn chorus sings out to greet the new day
Vibrant colors of sunrise dance across the Deschutes
As fishermen cast to where their fish play

The golf course then shakes itself awake
And golf carts start to roll with full force
Golfers swing on tee after tee
White spheres arc their way down the course

Joggers and bikers snake their way down the trails
"On your left" is their frequent cry
Children, helmets tilted, shout out with glee
As the sun climbs high in the sky

Screams of joy from the swimming pools
Bathers working hard on their tan
Hikers, returning from a long summer trek
Rafters slowly baked pink by the sun.

Then as the cool evening air moves in
With geese sillouetted by the setting sun
People rest on their decks and let their cares ebb away
Ah Sunriver!! Summer can be so much fun!

* * * * * *

TO OUR BELL RINGERS

By

Annis Oetinger

Bells of joy

Ring out with gladness,

Speak to us of happiness,

Tell us, Hear the golden chimes

Give harmony to every soul.

All hands move as notes direct,

Each tone in its proper place,

Give to all the melody now.

Gladden hearts who hear the song.

WILD LIFE IN SUNRIVER

By

Jack MacDonald

Wild life is abundant in Sunriver. You can see most of it from the comfort of your easy chair. Just look out your window.

We have a bird feeder filled with sunflower seeds in our back yard. It's a fast food stop for a variety of birds. A flock of Black Headed Grosbeaks will fly in and cover the feeder. After a bit they will fly off and a few Crossbills will arrive for a snack. Cassin Finches also frequent the feeder. Chickadees, Oregon Juncos and Nuthatches fly to the feeder, take one seed in their beaks and then fly into an adjacent tree. There they will crack open the sunflower seed, eat it and fly down for another one.

Blue Jays stop by now and then. They seem to be the bullies of the song bird world. All other birds take off when the Jays arrive.

Gray Jays visit us also. They frequent the tops of the large Ponderosa Pines but do not visit the bird feeder. Mourning Doves feed on the ground around the feeder as do Mountain Quail. The Quail are my favorite birds. When they pair off in the spring, the male will sit on a stump or rock and act as a sentinel while the female feeds. Later, when they bring their brood of ten or more little chicks around, he still acts as a lookout while the brood hunts for food.

Robins are plentiful here. They love to eat the berries on the Oregon Grape bushes and Mountain Ash trees as well as dig for their favorite worms.

A pair of Red Tailed Hawks nest in a Ponderosa Pine

tree not far from our house. They can be seen soaring on the air currents looking for prey such as squirrels and chipmunks.

The main scavengers of the airways here are the Crows. They are quick to make a meal on any road kill that happens in the area.

With all our trees, you know we have Woodpeckers. The most prevalent is the Red Shafted Flicker. We watched a pair raise two chicks not far from our house. Red Breasted Sapsuckers, White Headed Woodpeckers and Hairy Woodpeckers can also be seen in the Sunriver trees.

The last two years a Tree Swallow nested in the exhaust vent to our laundry room. When the exhaust fan was on, the birds must have thought a storm was brewing.

I heard a strange sound the other evening while filling the bird feeder. It went Brr Brr Brr UMPH. I heard it twice more before I realized what was causing it. A Night Hawk flying a hundred feet above the trees would dive for insects. At the end of its dive, the air rushing by its body as it turned up was causing this strange sound. The Night Hawk consumes a large quantity of the resident insects in Sunriver.

The many ponds on the Meadows and Woodland golf courses are home to a great number of waterfowl. Most prominent is the Canada Goose. They nest on the islands in the ponds. In the spring the proud parents escort the young goslings on the ponds with the goose in front and the gander bringing up the rear. They remind me of two battleships with a dozen or so destroyers in between. When the young geese are able to fly, the parents take them on short flights to teach them how to fly in formation.

Mallard Ducks also frequent these ponds as well as a few Cinnamon Teal.

Several Bald Eagles have nested in a tall dead tree near

the Deschutes River. These birds are often seen soaring in the skies above the meadow next to the Meadows golf course.

Besides birds, many mammals make Sunriver their home. Fresh water Otter have been seen in the ponds of both the Meadows and Woodlands golf courses. They come from the Deschutes River looking for some easy fish to catch.

Our dogs were barking at something from their kennel the other evening. I went to inspect, and a large raccoon ran out of our workshop. I had left the door open. I closed the door after the raccoon had run off. The next morning the raccoon was in our yard. I thought it strange that it was still there. When I opened the storage room door I was confronted with two half grown raccoons. It all became clear. Mother raccoon was here to retrieve her two young ones. I shooed them out with a broom and the three united by climbing to the top of a nearby pine tree.

Porcupines love the bark of young pine trees. Once in awhile you can see one having lunch in the branches of a tree.

The squirrel family is well represented in Sunriver. Chipmunks, Golden Mantles, Pine Squirrels and the beautiful Gray Squirrel are very plentiful. The Gray Squirrels love to take over the bird feeders. It is a constant challenge to erect the perfect bird feeder that is squirrel-proof. The Gray squirrels build a large nest high in a large Ponderosa Pine. The young are born and raised in the nest. When they first appear in the yard, they are already nearly full grown.

Mice and ground squirrel populations in the meadows are held in check by the Coyote. You can see Coyotes almost every day hunting for these rodents. The coyotes

91

roam all over Sunriver however, and have been known to make a dinner from an unsuspecting cat or small dog running loose.

My favorite wild life in Sunriver are our Mule Deer. They are beautiful animals. We had a herd of nineteen walk through our yard last spring. Lately a three-point buck has been bedding down under the neighbor's deck. One morning I was out for a walk and came upon a herd of five bucks on a little hill. They were all large animals with antlers running from three to five points. My wife and I named the hill "Buck" hill. Ironically, I haven't seen a buck on "Buck Hill" since.

WHERE SHALL WE LIVE

The She-Half of a Dialogue

By
Annis Oetinger

Don't talk to me about not being satisfied here. You're the one who didn't want to go on to Canada like we've always done before. Why should we spend all the time and effort going that far when everything is so great here – that's what you said. Now you're complaining ⸺

No, I never said that. You're forgetting. I thought we should do what we've done before, just like all the family has done simply forever, but you said this looked so green with plenty of water and plenty of company. And I'll grant you that. There's certainly plenty of company. Talk about extended families! Some of these people don't know when to quit. I ask you – twelve children. That's a bit much, don't you think. And some of those adolescents – so ill-mannered, pairing off so young and then squawking and fighting with others over where they're going to settle down. Some of the other neighbors too. You let them crowd you away from the best territory. You should do a better job of telling them off. You're too easy-going. Just because we weren't here last year doesn't mean we don't have rights. ⸺

Oh, yes, I certainly agree with you about these other two-legged creatures here. They are pretty weird with those useless, skinny wings and those odd sticks they swing around. And have you noticed – some of them don't seem to be able to walk very far. They stand up and swing that stick and then jump in a seat that rides them along. Those little round eggs they follow, too. Those things are dangerous. Did you see that wife who was hit by one last week? Poor thing can hardly walk. I hate to think what might happen if one hit a child. It could be killed. Very careless these creatures are. They act as if they own the place, and we don't belong here.

You're right that everything isn't perfect here, but then, where is? Certainly Canada wasn't so terrific, and I'm the first to say so. The food supply wasn't always to my liking, and there were more four-legged creatures skulking around just waiting to grab one of the kids. Some years it was too wet and some years too dry. Here it's green all the time since those rain things come on every night. Makes the grass just the way I like it best. I don't even mind sharing the area with those silly ducks. You have to watch out for an occasional cat or maybe a coyote, of course, but you're a good guard.

You're so right, and you know what I've been thinking? We decided we didn't want to fly all those extra hundreds of miles to Canada this summer. Now I'm thinking – why fly down south this winter? Why don't we just stay here all year? We've found ourselves a little paradise.

DINING OUT IS FOR THE BIRDS

By
Frank Allen

One of the joys of winter is watching the variety of birds that call Sunriver their home or are just passing through. People have discovered they get more watching of feathered friends if they set the right kind of table for their guests.

Bird feeders come in different sizes and shapes. They can be as simple as a pie pan, elegant as a work of art, but should be complex enough to discourage furry interlopers. The best ones are placed on poles, in trees, on fences or even stuck on windowsills. Four star menus at these outdoor dining rooms will list millet, black sunflower seeds, cracked corn, shelled peanuts, wheat and other grains.

Color, size, wing markings and voices identify different bird families and subgroups. Commonly seen dining in Sunriver are red crossbills, pine siskins, Cassin's finches, American gold finches and the occasional evening grosbeak. Evening grosbeaks came in droves until a few years ago when a virus caught up with a high percentage of them.

Larger birds include woodpeckers, robins, doves, and blackbirds. Stellar jays, redwing black birds, northern flickers and the Clark's nutcrackers are also frequent visitors. Small birds include mountain chickadees, pine siskins, humming-birds, and pygmy and white breasted nuthatches.

Birds have differing habits, flight patterns and actions. Nuthatches, for example, walk down the trunk of a tree headfirst Stellar jays will eat from a corn cob but they prefer peanuts snatched from lidded squirrel feeder.

Bird pecking orders are apparent both within and be-tween breeds. An evening grosbeak will shoulder a weaker bird off his perch. A jay will back away from a nutcracker. Most birds seem to prefer sunflower seed, but dried corn on the cob will attract Stellar jays and Clark's nutcrackers. I have watched two Jays remove all the kernels from an ear of corn in less than an hour. They flew off with kernels and hid them someplace nearby. A few days later, I found chips and splinters of cedar on the ground alongside the house. Overhead, on the roof, I found the jays had stashed some of their corn under shingles. Squirrels smelled the lode and were mining the shingles to reach the hidden treasure.

A feeder located near or under the protective branches of a tree will attract more birds than a feeder located 10 feet away. Small birds prefer flitting from a tree to a closeby feeder where predators have a difficult time picking them off. They pick a seed or two and then flit back to a protected branch to remove the husk and eat the seed. Larger birds will sit on a perch and eat continuously, as do squirrels.

It is not unreasonable to dispense more than 25 pounds of birdseed a month. Locate your feeders over shrubbery areas where the hulls will become mulch and so you can see birds easily from a window or a deck.

In cold weather, birds love suet and other high calorie kitchen fats. A good mixture is bacon fat, peanut butter, fat drippings from a roast, crushed egg shells plus bird seed. Add suet trimmed from beef, lamb or pork. If the above ingredients are placed in a plastic sandwich bag, and then carefully mixed by kneading, they make a neat package to place in a wire cage suet feeder. Harden the suet cakes in the freezer after preparing, and rip plastic bags off the suet cake before placing in the cage, in *cold weather*. We don't want birds to get scraps of the torn plastic in their gizzards. Hang suet cages containing the above mixtures in the shade out of direct sunlight. Like snowmen, they can melt.

SOMETHING HAPPENED ON THE WAY TO THE FIRE

By
R.C. Antle

Then something happened on the way to the fire!

The Aubrey Fire and nearby conflagrations scared the hell out of the Sunriver Homeowner's Board. It could happen here! Our police chief warned, "There will be deaths, plenty of them if a fire occurs here." So an elaborate evacuation plan was drafted. Volunteers were organized. They practiced their part in the scheme, setting up signs~ "This way Out". A telephone system was designed to alert, and a post was assigned to each volunteer. The homeowner board established a six year plan to thin our forests and eliminate ladder fuel. Finally, six sirens were installed to warn the inhabitants and visitors of an impending disaster.

Cutting trees or eradicating undergrowth in our forests was heresy to the old-timers. Let me tell you why.

Almost thirty years ago two gentlemen from up Portland way discovered along the banks of the Deschutes river, a tract of land called Camp Abbott. During World War II troops were trained here. This idyllic property so entranced these men that a resort was developed and it became Sunriver, named for a small stream that ran through it before emptying into the Deschutes River.

The theme of Sunriver was *au naturel*, or for us common folk, keep it rustic. The spell was cast! Slowly, cabins were built and the carefree life~a little fishin', some huntin', a stroll in the woods, but mostly just relaxing and watching the wildlife, was the day's task. The only thinking done was who had the right-of-way at the infamous circles.

With growth, rules were established to keep the land the way God had intended. Every tree, every limb, every bush was sacred. No cutting without good reason ... and good reasons were inordinately difficult to obtain. Slowly but surely, like any plague, the "locust" arrived from the south. Homes squashed the lots, trees had to go, lawns appeared. The rules however persisted.

The Nature Center was appointed "custodian" of the edicts that kept Sunriver a wooded paradise. The efforts of a few who wouldn't fall in line got the "custodians attention, pronto. I remember old Roger the Logger, who would march out, ax in hand, greet his neighbors, and promptly level an offending pine that obscured his view of the Mountain That Never Married. An incident that rankled the custodians of power was the fella who weekended lying in his recliner, guffawing at the sadomasochistic would be golfers attempting to extricate themselves from a deep bunker. When the growing forest obscured his picture-window view of those characters playing in the sand, he toppled thirty-five evergreens.

Recently, I, too, got the attention of nature's saviors. We were building a new home on a lot blessed with adjacent common ground, which contained several dead trees, slash from previous cuttings and ugly litter. The trees were a threat, so I contacted the custodians. They sent a man with a pink slip that not only gave me permission to cut dead trees but also the necessity to eliminate sixty percent of the "ladder fuel".

That sent me into a tizzy. Not being a man of the forest, I found the term ladder fuel an enigma. My trusty "Webster" and several other heavy tomes hiding in our Homeowner library did not contain the term. Fortunately a serendipitous meeting with an old forester, put me straight. "That's all those bushes, especially under trees, all that crap swallowing our forests." He pointed out several species, Squaw current, Rabbitbush, and "The worst is Bitterbrush--the ice cream plant of deer, it's pesky. It also includes dead lower branches of trees that can act like a ladder."

Armed with saw, clippers and mattock (loaned by a friend), I began my grubbing. It is an activity that I came by honestly. You see my dad often spent Sunday afternoons grubbing and burning in the lot next to our home. In fact he scorched our house pretty good one day.

So with tools in hand I went to work. It's hard work, too. I wished I were younger. But after I spent many days on my knees, pulling, cutting and tugging, the lot looks mighty nice.

Who says you can't teach an old dog new tricks? I now am an expert on ladder fuel. My home is safer and Sunriver is safer. I, as one of those volunteers, don't want to be out there with my sign--This Way Out--directing traffic.

It is up to each of us to eliminate ladder fuel! Help make Sunriver safe!

SQUIRRELS

By
Keith S. Pennington

The squirrels that live along Abbot Drive

Play chicken with cars and survive

It's the "Survival of the Fit"

Just the way Darwin said it.

At least for those still alive!!

LOTTI

By
Dave Ghormley

Every year someone comes out with a new bird feeder designed to feed birds but not squirrels, and every year the squirrels and the chipmunks figure how to chase the birds off and gorge on the bird seed. Now, the Bird Feeder Makers Association should know that their latest effort fails, too, but not because of the squirrels.

You see, my wife bought us a new feeder from a shop in the Mall, and we thought that we finally had the answer. It had a giant plastic dome, and every time a big old gray squirrel tried to shinny down the chain and get to the birdseed, he'd bounce off the dome and end up on his head on the ground. Great! Just what we needed. Right? Wrong!

The squirrels recruited some help. They talked a big old doe, who hangs around our back yard and whom we've named Lotti, to tilt the seed holder up and let the seeds pour out onto the ground. But they may have been too smart for their own good.

The problem the squirrels are having is that Lotti's going back on her deal with them. She's finding out something that a lot of us already know- that nuts go well when you sprinkle them on the top of a salad. She already knows that the latest thing in salad cuisine is to top off the greens with a few flowers. She's been cleaning us out of petunias and pansies as fast as we can grow them for some time. But now she's learned that she can drain the new bird feeder every night with no problem and poke all of those good sunflower seeds down on top of the petunias in her big fat stomach!

As far as the squirrels are concerned, this is not cool. It's downright greedy. They're ready to declare war, and I don't blame them.

I don't know what to do about all of this. I can certainly sympathize with Lotti that a steady diet of petunias and pansies must get pretty boring, but, on the other hand, she's such a glutton that my other friends, the birds and the squirrels, are getting pretty gaunt. A few have even moved away and are over at the neighbor's, where they are finding that the feeding is better.

All I can figure is that we need a "deer and squirrel proof" feeder. But this is a whole new dimension. This may not arrive until the new millennium! If it ever is developed, it will be a truly unbelievable invention- at least on the order of the Pentium chip. But there is a real risk that no such device can be developed. After all, trying to make a bird feeder squirrel <u>and</u> deer proof is asking quite a bit!

I've got it! I'm going to load that feeder up with chili-pepper-flavored sunflower seeds and then make sure that the deer get them, not the squirrels and birds. If that works, I'll bet I can sell tons of "Hot Pepper Seeds"!

However, I'm not sure how to be sure Lotti gets them first! Hmm.

WINTER COMING

By
Annis Oetinger

Push the days back, back into summer.

Winter is coming before I am ready.

Bring back the warmth, the sunshine and blue sky,

The days with a face toward tomorrow.

Too soon the cold and the dark will be here.

Forever

THE RIVER OTTERS IN SUNRIVER.

By

Glen Bending

The Deschutes River meanders along the border of Sunriver. Sometimes it flows briskly past large homes and parkland and after leaving Sunriver it becomes a turbulent challenge for the white water rafters.

Many Brown, Rainbow, and Brook Trout inhabit the clear waters and the Otter are prominent fishers. These large, playful animals can be seen at any time along the banks, and, occasionally, they may be seen sliding precipitately down the shore where they splash and tumble into the water.

One unusually cold winter day the section of the river in front of the Trout House restaurant was frozen except for about 20 circular holes in the ice. Large dark brown Otters kept popping up to breathe and to climb up on the ice surface where they ate their catches of Trout with obvious signs of enjoyment. The Otters can also be seen at the nearby High Desert Museum but it was thrilling to see them frolicking about in their wild state 20 to 50 feet away directly below the large picture windows of a busy restaurant in broad daylight.

The Otters seem to be increasing in number but they have not spoiled the fishing for their competing human fishermen and the resident bald eagles who also fish these waters.

MORE THAN A GOOD WALK SPOILED

By
Robert C. Antle

I am an inveterate golfer. In polite circles I'd be called a golf nut. When I retired to Sunriver in 1987, I jumped right into the golf scene by joining the Sunriver Men's Golfing Club.

Foursomes, consisting of players of varied handicaps, compete weekly. The games played vary as much as the abilities of the individuals. Typically the handicaps might be 10, 18, 25, and 36. A thirty-sixer, might be a 28 in disguise--if he cheated, or a 56, a rank beginner. After introducing ourselves, crossing our drivers, as a pledge of unity, our captain (this distinguished honor is bestowed on the low handicapper), leads the troops to the first tee.

Each of us furtively studies the other's practice swing--so smooth, so graceful, but once the ball is teed, the muscles tighten, the backswing shortens, and trepidation overwhelms.

I remember Pete. He broke out a sleeve of new balls, slipped two into his rear pocket and proceeded to slice his first drive into the pond. Quickly he teed a second that went dead left into the woods. As he nervously set his third ball on its perch, I suggest, "Pete, why don't you use an old ball on this hole".

"I don't own an old ball."

One day old George, not a bad golfer, who prided himself upon his driving ability, led off for our team. Fidgety he addressed his ball, teed unusually high. With elan he swung his Big Bertha, posing on his follow through as his eyes searched the sky for his booming drive. But somehow, unbelievably the ball popped up and with a flump, fell behind him on the tee.

Struck dumb, we stood, silent, mouths gaping

"Where the hell did it go? In unison, we pointed, and then we broke into hilarious laughter.

I'll never forget one gentle man. He talked to his ball as he addressed it. "Nice little ball, go straight, stay out of trouble". Amusingly, he would glance over his shoulder a couple of times, as if something sinister lurked behind him. (His conversations must have worked because he consistently drove straight.)

One soggy morning, Bill, a good golfer, attempted to reach the green on a par five with his second shot, a three-wood. Bill had a tendency to hit down on the ball. On this occasion, the head of his club really dug into the turf. A foot of terra firma sprung forward, as if thrown from a shovel. All eyes pierced the mist, searching--did he do it? No one picked up the ball's flight. Strange, really bizarre. We looked down, could it be? One of the group dropped to his knees and followed a track with his fingers. Sure enough, like a mole, the ball was buried in the sod. Sheepishly, Bill said, "Does the imbedded ball rule apply"?

One of our men consistently parked his cart between his ball and his fellow players. He never had a bad lie. One day I noticed him kicking his ball forward. He used his instep like Pele. After three boots, he turned to his partner and asked, "Do you think I can reach the green with a four-wood?" "Not yet!"

Sandbagging is the label applied to a golfer who has an inflated handicap. Infamous Murphy, who was ambidextrous, sprouted a bloated handicap of 23. He played left-handed when he needed to shoot low--maybe in the low eighties. He could whack his two-iron farther than my drive. He won everything, except as my partner--when he never broke 110. We finally banished him to a distant golf club.

I'll never forget the morning I was paired with a man who marched the fairways like a wooden soldier--stiff and straight in slow time, his bag majestically draped on his square shoulder. We had begun in a drizzle and it was still raining. When our soldier came to his ball, he methodically removed his bag, stood it up using the attached stand and surveyed his next shot with great diligence. Removing the head-cover from his club, he balanced the cover upon the remaining clubs and with solemn deliberation placed his Sherlock Holmes pipe and then his dark glasses individually on this soft cushion he had devised. Wiping his hands, then his brow with a towel he drew from his hip pocket, he swung--but it was a practice swing, the first of two. He moved like a meal moving through a python. After finishing the tenth hole, I said, "Three hours is a long time for ten holes". Our Lieutentant countered, "We aren't holding anyone up". He was correct. The foursomes behind had all quit at the turn.

I love to retrieve balls from ponds. One morning I was out teetering on the pond's edge when a gust of wind blew my hat off and as I tried to catch it, I went kerplunk, head first, in the swan dive of the century, arms extended, my right hand clenching the ball retriever, my left clutching my hat. The geese, startled, scattered as if frightened by a coyote. I never knew if their squawking was in applause or derision.

A few years back I had a game everyone dreams about--drives straight, good irons and putts that found the cup, even a sixty-foot snake. When I reached the eighteenth tee of the Woodland's course one of my buddies, who was keeping score, remarked. "Buck, if you par this hole, you'll shoot your age."

How did he know I was seventy-three. No secrets in Sunriver. I was well aware of the situation. Every golfer aspires to shooting his age. His remark just added to the pressure.

My drive found the middle of the fairway, beyond the tree. Upon checking the yardage book, I was a hundred and fifteen yards from the flagstick, a perfect nine-iron. I selected the club took a big breath and attempted to take my backswing, As if encased in a block of ice, I froze, immobile. No backswing. I looked up. Stan, observing from his cart, grinned, amused at my predicament. I dropped my club and walked around his cart trying to relax. I snatched the club from the ground, thinking, how ridiculous. I took my stance and tried again. Impossible, no backswing! True Buck fever, I could not pull the trigger. By now Stan was bent over, trying not to laugh out loud. A noticeable silence prevailed. I sensed all were watching, waiting. Again I marched around the cart, I was angry with myself, embarrassed really.

I took my stance and somehow got the club back. Not a good shot, but the ball ended within a foot of the green. My nervous chip rolled to a couple of feet of the hole.. Stan kicked it back. I had done it, shot my age. The boys pounded my back, shook my hand~a true celebration. "Drinks are on me", I shouted.

In Sunriver golf is more than a good walk spoiled.

THE SUSTENANCE OF LIFE

By

Annis Oetinger and Mary Ellen Anderson

Sunriver is famous for many things - golf courses, bike paths, great scenery, good friends. What else? Think pot lucks and parties. You guessed it! Good Food. This good food is brought to you by the many inspired cooks, both men and women, who live here.

They've shared their favorite recipes in three cookbooks published by the Sunriver Women's Club. These books have benefited various charitable organizations in Central Oregon. The first book, beautifully hand-lettered, has become a collector's item. The second also has been sold out, and the third is nearing that status.

When the members of the group decided to publish a third book, it seemed sensible to try out the contributed recipes - to give them the all-important taste test. A committee was formed, and the members eagerly went about their work.

Soups were first on the list. Each committee member picked out a soup recipe. On a specified day we met with our soup pots in hand in Mary Ellen Anderson's spacious kitchen. Armed with bowls, spoons, pencil and paper we circled the stove tasting the different soups and carefully noting what we thought of each one. Too salty, too thin, too bland or maybe just right. By the time we'd judiciously sampled each variety, we relaxed in well-fed comfort to compare notes and to choose a recipe for the next session which was salads.

Oh, my, but some of those concoctions were good!

And some were "different". Canned stewed tomatoes with onion in raspberry Jello? Sounds weird but it turned out to be very tasty.

From salads we moved on to main dishes. You never thought there could be so many ways to fix chicken, did you? And all manner of new ideas for casseroles. That session left us feeling not just well-fed but totally stuffed.

The day we did desserts was a taster's dream day, a choc-o-holics heaven, the ultimate answer to a sweet tooth. Never before in the history of Sunriver has a group of serious recipe evaluators reveled in such yummy luxury. If the truth be known, it came close to being too much of a good thing. Did a sweet tooth person ever think he or she simply could not take another bite of any dessert, no matter how luscious it looked?

Lest anyone think this business of trying out recipes sounds like extremely enjoyable duty, there was work involved too. All the recipes had to be typed for the printer, and sometimes checked for accuracy. If your recipe said a dollop of butter or a dash of something, or a can of whatever, it must need to be reduced to a definite measurement. How much is a dollop - a tablespoon? A dash, maybe half a teaspoon, and what size can?

When the book finally was published, then the distribution committee went to work. Where do you put a few thousand books? Who will send out the letters to book-stores, then fill the orders that come back? And who will give the time to sit and sell books at various venues?

Central Oregon charities have benefited from the profits on these books, and thousands of households have enjoyed new recipes with the taste of Sunriver. It was work and effort for a good cause. But those who helped taste the recipes enjoyed it most.

PATHWAYS

By
Frank Allen

Walking is good exercise. It works the big muscles of the body as well as the heart and can work up a sweat. Ghengis Khan's troops, who conquered everybody in their time, were in good shape because the Khan required every soldier to run, walk or work hard enough each day to break a sweat.

Sunriver has 27 miles of bike paths and about 10 miles of golf cart paths. Residents and visitors with ambition to walk, jog or bike, use the paths all times of the year when they are not covered with snow. When there is enough snow, a few die-hards try to ski on the pathways but the berms of snow at each lane crossing make this difficult. The experienced do their Sunriver skiing on the golf course. Walkers and joggers can't resist using the golf cart paths but it is verboten and hazardous to your health in golf season. Most have the courtesy and smarts for their own safety to avoid cart paths when golfers are on the course. After all, the cart paths are for the golfers.

Walkers come in all types. There are those who walk, or run briskly to reach their goals. At the other extreme are those who decide that the dog needs some exercise and they stroll along for the walk. Bikers who ride slowly with their dog on a leash are in for a surprise when an impudent squirrel suddenly decides to cross the path. One lady walks along with a matched set of scotties. Couples walk together, sometimes each with a dog, matched or unmatched. Some walkers and joggers wear "Walkmans", radios with earphones so they can keep up on the news or listen to music. They may be so preoccupied they will not say hello as you pass.

The majority of people you meet on the paths will give you a hearty hello and a big smile.

Walkers and joggers come in all ages from skinny twelve year olds to wrinkled eighty year olds. Regular exercisers tend to be slim, trim and pleasing to eye. There are other kinds.

Walkers can cover about three or four miles in an hour. Joggers and runners will cover a lot more. One of the challenges is to vary the daily route so there is a minimum of repetition. You should realize a simple out and back on the same route is not bad because you notice different things going in the opposite direction. Loop routes are preferred and more interesting, and you get a different view the next time when you take the reverse direction. Unless you live on an edge of Sunriver, you can usually dream up a dozen interesting routes with a minimum of duplication.

You will notice different things while walking depending on your interests. There are gray squirrels, ground squirrels, deer, and coyotes. One also notices a new house here and a new house there, and houses that fit, and houses that don't seem to fit. The volunteers who pulled weeds months ago will notice patches of knapweed that were not picked up.

So plan your route, check the batteries in your "Walkman", select your most comfortable walking shoes and take off. Dress warmly in the winter and take a cane if you are a bit unsteady. Just try to stay out of the puddles, especially when they are frozen. You could land on your backside!

ON YOUR LEFT

By
Robert C. Antle

"Dad, are we lost again?"

The piercing voice which broke the silence of a beautiful August morning came from an eight year old girl who straddled her bike, waiting the decision of her father. They had stopped where the bike path forked. Dad held two maps, comparing them to the sign at circle nine. Which way? He wondered.

Karen, anxious, shook her head, her blond hair tumbling from beneath her red helmet, like a cascading waterfall. Her mother quietly spoke.

"We have all day. Patience, dear".

"But it happens every day, Mom".

"I want to see little dogs again", blurted David, a four year old, who pushed his bike back and forth, "Rung, rung", he growled, like a motor-cycle driver. His bike was equipped with training wheels

"They're prairie dogs, stupid", said Karen

"Now, dear, actually they are ground squirrels. I'm sure we'll see them. I've packed a lunch and we'll picnic along the river."

"I sure hope those horses gallop again, that's cool", said David, who was dressed in droopy shorts and a Mickey Mouse tee shirt. He had roared his bike up next to the trailer hitched cleverly to his dad's bike. Their small mongrel dog, Mitch, who enjoyed riding around like a maharaja, occupied the trailer. "Nice Mitch", David petted his pal. Mitch licked the small hand.

"I think I've got it figured out." Dad beamed, confidently.

"On your left" came a loud voice, as four bikers thundered by, narrowly missing David.

Off they biked following their intrepid father who was devoting a week to a family vacation. This was the second trip to Sunriver for the Kendricks from Kent, Washington. Although Dad would love to play a game of golf, he enjoyed biking with mom and the youngsters, especially over the twenty-seven miles of trails provided for vacationers. The landscape was refreshing and there was a sense of tranquillity, but best of all one was never too far from a drink or snack. It beat camping. When the children tired one could escape to the condo they had rented.

The Kendricks stopped at the Cardinal bridge. Some ducks bobbed in the river, diving and drifting about.

"Hey, look at that" exclaimed Karen.

"What is it?" questioned David as he squirmed between his parents to catch a look.

"Water snakes" "Where, Where? Gosh, they squirt fast", the excited boy jumped up and down on the railing.

"Hey, what's that skinny thing", David pointed to a heron.

"He sure doesn't eat much." That brought quite a laugh from his parents. Dad ruffled his son's red hair.

"Best we move on. Find a nice spot for lunch." Dad did like to eat.

The horses were out and the ground squirrels gave the bikers quite a show. Some darted about, some stood on their hind legs, viewing the landscape while the more timid peeped out of their holes. They were fun to observe. Dad attempted to explain the intricate network of tunnels and lairs beneath the surface.

They lunched along the Deschutes, in a shady coppice of

small trees. Dad relaxed on a blanket while Mom arranged all the goodies. David jumped dad and was tossed in the air like a dry leaf, wind blown. Even Mitch participated, chasing birds that pecked along the riverbank. Just prior to handing Dad his sandwich and drink, Mom stooped over and kissed her husband.

"I love you"

Refreshed and eager for more, they raced on. David got out ahead but soon his sister passed him in typical sibling rivalry. They stopped and fed some geese that lingered near a pond. As they approached the Sun River near the lodge, they noticed a small group of people gathered on and near the bridge, so they stopped.

"What is it?"

"Otters.", a lady answered.

The bikes strewn nearby, the excited youngsters crowded into the fascinated group. David and Karen crawled to the bank of the stream that was covered with duckweed.

Enthralled, the children watched as the whiskered play-mates dived and reappeared to survey the surroundings unaware that their yellowed snouts added to the amusement of their fans. David grabbed his sister in pure exhilaration, his face full of joy and amazement. Finally the performers dived and disappeared. The show was over. Some of the spectators even clapped.

As the Kendricks rode back to condo, still exclaiming the delight of the otter scene, David remarked, "Hey, Dad, can we go to Goody's?"

HEARD ON THE GOLF COURSE
Among Some of the Athletically Challenged Ladies
(those with High Handicaps)

By
Annis Oetinger

- Oh, good shot! (her drive is more or less in the middle of the fairway barely on the short grass.)
- That's not where I aimed! (the ball is far left under a tree)
- Not in the sand again! (every bunker jumps up and grabs her ball)
- These greens are really fast today. (she putted the ball ten feet past the hole)
- That's the nicest sound in golf. (the ball finally clunked in the bottom of the hole)
- That wind is fierce! (the ball went straight up in the air)
- Do you have a retriever? I think I can see my ball here in the water. (every water hazard reaches out and swallows her ball)
- This rough is really rough! (that's why it's called rough)
- That was kind of a grounder. (it sure scared a few worms as it went by)
- It helps if I keep my eye on the ball. (she managed this time to keep from looking up before the club actually hit the ball)
- Well, it's a beautiful day anyway. (her score is mounting up rapidly)
- Hey, I nearly got a birdie! (poor robin came close to getting smeared)
- You're still away. (the saddest words in golf)
- Eighty yards? That's an awkward distance for me. (any

distance is awkward for her)
- I went clear over the green. Why do I get all the yardage when I don't need it? (unfortunately there is no way to save that extra yardage for another shot)
- You mean I have to count those putts you gave me? (welcome to the real world, sweetie.)
- WOW! (she hit a GOOD one)
- Anybody would think we knew how to play this game. (everyone in the foursome managed to get off the tee in reasonably respectable fashion)
- The golf may not be great, but it beats cleaning the kitchen. (the kitchen can wait until winter.)
- And our thought for the day – Golf is a game where the player tries to put a small white ball into a smaller hole with implements totally unsuited to the task.

FALL IN SUNRIVER

By
Keith S Pennington

The sunshine feels warm upon the skin
But the mountain breeze carries a brief chill
Summer is felt in these golden rays
While Winter jogs our memories still

Most tourists have left for other climes
Only a small contingent now remain
To walk the trails on clear autumn days
And hear trees whistle to the wind's refrain

Tall Ponderosa gently rock the cradle
As the Earth slowly falls asleep
Golden Aspen leaves hush the ground into silence
On the trails beneath our feet.

The Sisters then put on lace petticoats of snow
While Bachelor slowly turns white as from fright
The Deschutes: It just goes with the flow
As the days slowly turn into nights

The crystal clear days and the cool nights
Birds flocking to obey nature's call
Deer putting on their winter coats
Ahh! Autumn! Another Sunriver fall

SEPTEMBER SONG

By
Annis Oetinger

Fog in the morning, then sunshine,
Less heat in the sun than July.
The breeze that twirls the leaves on the aspens
    Is sometimes warm, left over from summer,
    Then chilly foretelling winter to come.
Quiet days to savor, fewer cars, bicycles, people.
Vacation season is over, school has started.
The buck who comes to drink from my birdbath has lost
    The velvet on his antlers, the fawns are half as big as
    Momma now, and their spots are fading.
Rabbitbush is turning gold, taking the light from the sun
    As it sinks lower in the sky.
White clouds feather across the blue sky, white like snow.
Beautiful days of September, linger long in this place

IT BEATS PLAYING SOLITAIRE
By
Robert C. Antle

"Hey Joe, how about running for the Board."
Joe scurries across the street. "What Board, Frank?"
"The Homeowner's Board.

"Are you crazy! Haven't been retired two years yet and you want me to take that thankless position. Hell, I served on so many boards down in Pasadena, I felt like a carpenter. Church, bank, country club, I've done it all."

"You're just the man. Lots of experience."

"I'm experienced enough to know I don't want cranks calling all hours or being carped at by some gadfly who'll sit in the front row of every meeting."

"Sure we have a few, but by and large, the community supports us. Give it some thought. It sure beats playing Solitaire."

It seems that every president, sometime during his term tells the citizens of our country about the importance of volunteerism. "People have to help each other; government cannot do it all."

If the bigwigs in Washington would look outside the beltway they would realize that America runs on volunteers. Sunriver is a prime example.

Residents of Sunriver come to escape the nightmarish life of the big city--to enjoy the recreational facilities and to live the quiet life with new friends. Soon, active individuals seek outlets for their talents. One can ski just so many days, or play so many rounds of golf. Sunriver offers many opportunities for the energies of her people. They volunteer. It could be working on the musical festival--a major project, or reading to children at the Three River School, arranging tennis, golf or card games, or serving on the library board, Sunriverites serve and enjoy. Volunteers make Sunriver the fine community that it is.

"Frank", Joe sips his mocha at a local coffee shop. " I've been thinking the past few months about your suggestion; running for the Homeowner Board. My golf games in good shape, I've worn out two decks playing Solitaire, in fact, I beat old Sol about fifty percent of the time, and besides Myrtle thinks I should get out of the house more often."

"Beat old Sol half the time! Do you cheat?"

"Not really, but Dave Ghormley gave me some good pointers."

"Joe, that is great news. I'll get you all the info on running for the board. You won't regret it."

* * * * * *

GOLF IN SUNRIVER

by
Keith S. Pennington

There was a young man from LA

Who liked to hunt and play golf each day

On Sunriver's North Course

He hit his ball with full force

And got a "Goose-in-one", so they say.

120

SUNRIVER WOMENS' CLUB TWENTY-FIFTH ANNIVERSARY

By
Annis Oetinger

In 1998 the Sunriver Womens' Club marked the twenty-fifth anniversary of its founding. Sheri Allis, who helped start the organization and was the first president, reminisced about the early years.

"There weren't many of us here. One day we decided Sunriver should have a women's club. We had a meeting in the Great Hall. I think there were maybe thirty of us."

For the first pot luck dinner in the Great Hall, the members did it all. They did the set-up and brought the food. "We could cook there twenty years ago, and there was no charge for the use of the hall."

There were magical musical programs by candle light arranged by Teresa and Jay Bowerman.

In the first three years the Women's Club directed much of their energy towards becoming knowledgeable and involved in Emergency Medical Care for the community. Life sustaining equipment was purchased for the First Aid Department. A class in CPR was offered, and 60 people came.

In 1974 seventeen more women joined the club, and in 1976 the first fund raising events were held. A fashion show, soup supper and Tasting Party raised enough money that the Women's Club was able to donate over $1000 to the United Fund.

A spaghetti dinner featuring Dick Miller's secret sauce recipe was held in 1977. Three hundred people were served netting more than $700. Naomi Barton was membership chairman, and the group had grown to 131 members. On a motion by Karin Rundberg, the club began keeping committee reports.

In 1979 the first Sunriver cookbook was published thanks to Betty Kobey. It has now become a collector's item cherished by those lucky enough to have a copy.

That year saw the beginning of a dream - a community center for Sunriver. The Women's Club deposited money into a special fund for furnishings for the center. We're all still dreaming, and the money in the fund has been growing with accumulated interest all these years.

Between the years of 1977 and 1984 Emergency Medical Care continued to be a focus for fund raising. Donations totaling $6534 enabled our Department of Public Safety to purchase heart monitors, two-way portable radios, the Jaws of Life equipment and training materials.

In 1980 the Sunriver Women's Club began to reach out into the surrounding community. Jean Dillard organized the members who wished to donate their time to the developmentally disabled.

Beth Wright held the first Newcomers Outreach for new residents in 1982. The first club newsletter was published in 1983. The 1980's saw the start of the annual Welcome Tea to give women new to the community a chance to become acquainted.

Sheri Allis and the other members of that small original group can be proud of what they started. Those thirty women have grown to more than 225, the outreach programs now include scholarships, the Nature Center, the Sunriver Music Festival, our Library, Three Rivers School and many programs to assist the needy in the surrounding area. Our thanks go to the charter members of the Sunriver Women's Club and the legacy they have left for us.

S.R.O.A.

By
Lois Earley

The S.R.O.A. office is, by definition, the mayor's office of Sunriver. This office oversees and maintains the Police Department, the Public Works Department, Fleet Services Department, the Recreation Department, Design Review and Accounting. Also under this umbrella is the 'Sunriver Scene' office. With all these departments and employees, the General Manager's position is not an easy one. The manager works closely with the Board of Directors who ultimately set the policies and standards. The office is always a busy place. However, the employees usually can find time for a little levity.

Executive Privilege

Whose idea was this anyway? It was still dark and cold, and here I was loading a toilet into the trunk of my car, instead of sleeping. But time was of the essence since everything had to be in place before the office opened at 8 o'clock.

I huffed and puffed but finally got the toilet loaded into my car, then sped off into the darkness. Thank goodness there were only two or three cars in the parking lot this time of morning. The unloading process was easier (I suppose because I didn't want to be recognized by anyone). This time there was a flight of steps to ascend! Up the steps, unlock the door, through the General Manager's office and onto his balcony. The major prop was now in place.

I reported for work, nice and tidy and on time. As other

123

employees came in, so other items arrived. Magazine rack equipped with publications, tissue roll, telephone and Big Ashtray (for cigars). The finishing touch: above the commode an elaborate sign: EXECUTIVE WASHROOM.

The General Manager arrived. Everyone watched breathlessly as he entered his office. He looked suspicious, but said nothing.

After awhile, he walked out onto his balcony to smoke a cigar (something he swore he never did). The whispers passed through the office quickly and bodies gathered hastily to see the reaction to his employees' handiwork.

At first he seemed to ponder the scene, then came the outburst of laughter. He did not disappoint the office staff. But then, the office staff did not disappoint him either.

The Birthday Party

Prior to the executive washroom episode, the office staff arranged a surprise birthday party for another General Manager. Everyone from Public Works, Fleet Services, Fire and Police Departments arrived a little before 8 A.M. Office personnel arrived, unlocked the office and turned on the lights and computers, started a pot of coffee and then left.

After the stage was set, the office staff and employees from the other departments met under the General Manager's balcony. It was hard to keep everyone hushed until a lookout told us that the manager had just arrived on the scene. Then everyone was quiet as quiet can be.

The manager climbed the steps to the office, entered and found the entire office deserted. We all waited patiently under the balcony. Finally one of the men from Public Works called the manager to the phone. He told the manager there was a problem at the ice rink next door and would he come to the balcony so they could talk. The manager opened the balcony door and stepped out.

At that time everyone emerged beneath the balcony and hollered 'Surprise", and was he ever! His retort was "You are all fired". Of course no one took him seriously, but we all hastened back into the office. He said we really had him fooled-it was like everyone came to work and then was whisked away by aliens or something equally as bizarre. That made the day start on a happy note for everyone.

* * * * * *

SKIING

by
Keith S. Pennington

There was once a skier from New York

Whose skiing was not as good as his talk.

While out skiing Bachelor's bump

He flipped twice and fell on his rump.

So he claimed he'd taken up ski-flying for sport!

WINTER IN SUNRIVER

By
Keith S. Pennington

The Lodge at night, all covered in white
It's lights piercing the dark
Snow drifting slowly through the pines
Adding icing to branch and bark
Snow piled high along the drives
Houses snuggling in their blankets of snow
Mall lights beckoning like beacons of hope
Cars spinning their wheels to go
Golf course lakes all covered with ice
Bike trails layered with snow
People hunched against winter's cold
Enjoying Sunriver's winter glow

Skiers leaving after first light
To sample the night's powder fall
Hot tubs whirring as the sun goes down
Muscles straining as they walk to the Mall
Foggy windows in the Pizzaria
Down coats on bench and wall
Restaurant lights beckoning to the crowds
As they make their way through the Mall.
The smell of wood burning fires in the night
Boots squealing across frozen snow
Lovers holding hands on frozen trails they walk
Enjoying Sunriver's winter show.

DEEP POWDER

By
Dave Hennessey

Rrrrrrrrrrrr - sleepy hand groped to silence the alarm. It's 5:00 a.m. and pitch dark. "Why do I do this to myself," I thought. "No one gets up this early, not in Sunriver, especially now that we're retired." I stumbled to the patio door and pulled back the curtains.

"What's it doing?" Came a sleepy voice from under a pile of quilts.

"It's 16 degrees and there looks like ten inches of fresh snow on the deck."

I reached for the phone and dialed 382-7888 for the 5:oo a.m. Mt. Bachelor ski report. "Good morning, skiers and boarders, this is Matt with your 5 o'clock ski report. Twenty-eight inches of snow fell overnight, total accumulation is 240 inches at mid-mountain. Temperature is 13 degrees, winds are light. Mt. Bachelor has nine lifts operating————."

"Sounds like a great powder day. Let's go skiing."

"I've got work to do," Came the reply from under the covers.

"You can work any time. Fresh, deep powder snow has priority. I bet the Maleys will be going up. We'll take lunch and meet the Sunriver gang at Pine Martin Lodge."

"You guys can ski the powder. Dottie and I will ski the groomed."

Dawn was breaking as we drove up Forest Road 45. The early sunrays falling on the snow covered old growth, ponderosa pines turning the landscape into a magical winter wonderland.

When we arrived at West Village, snow was everywhere. Mammoth trucks were pushing it across the parking lot while a huge snow thrower belched a stream of white high into the air above the already towering snow piles. Sallie and I hiked up the cat track to the ski patrol room to check in and pick up a radio. At the bottom of the Pine Martin lift we could barely see the top of the mountain.

"It looks like Thunderbird has been groomed," Sallie said pointing uphill.

"Isn't that Joe coming down Egan? Dottie is right behind him."

"This is great," exclaimed Joe as he slid to a stop.

"It doesn't get any better than this. Where do you want to ski?"

"Anywhere. You lead. Take us to those hidden places where all you ski patrol guys go for good face shots."

"Okay, we'll ski the Outback. I know a couple of runs through the trees. Sallie, I think you and Dottie might want to stay on the front side. This could be tough skiing."

We got on the chair lift and headed up the mountain. At the top we chanced to meet Si Reedy and Ross Williams, a friend from Sun Valley, Idaho.

"Si, We're going to the Outback. Come and join us."

"I'm all for it, but Ross didn't bring his fat skis."

"Dave is skiing on skinny skis. I'm sure Ross won't have any problems," chimed Joe.

I changed radio frequencies, advised dispatch, and assumed my position at the head of these intrepid skiers. With a push of my ski poles I dropped into a shallow gully that would take us to the Outback. It was snowing lightly. As we skied away from the lodge, it became quiet. The only sound was a soft, muffled swish as the skis glided through the cold, untracked snow. The snow billowed up around my ankles, light and fluffy. "Perfect, just perfect," I said to myself.

I slid to a stop at the top of Down Under West. Joe, Si and Ross were right behind me. "The run I have in mind is off to the left about 100 yards down the hill. Keep each other in sight. We don't want to lose anyone."

Over the edge I went. Check-turn, check-turn, the snow billowed up around my knees. I balanced myself over the center of my skis, the K-2's responding beautifully. One turn after another I followed the contours of the terrain. Over a rise, into a depression, over a bump, down the hill I flew. I felt like I was floating on air. All too soon I was at the bottom.

I looked back up the hill. Joe, Si and Ross were halfway down, the rhythm of their turning was synchronized. It was wonderful to watch, three neatly carved tracks on a field of white.

"Let's do that again!" Joe said, panting for breath. Exhilaration showed on their faces.

"Don't worry, there's plenty more ahead," I assured them.

We made three more runs through the little glades that dot the Outback. The intrepid skiers were doing well.

"I'm good for one more run," exclaimed Si. "Let's go over to the Northwest area."

"Okay, we've got time before we meet the Sunriver gang for lunch. There are some nice bowls west of Sparks Lake run."

Whopped on the Northwest Connection lift for a smooth ride to the new Northwest Express lift. Two miles from bottom to top, the ride took 10 minutes.

On top the clouds thickened. Visibility was going

down. "Keep close. The snow is drifting and with reduced visibility, skiing will be tricky."

We crossed over the ridge and dropped into the West bowl. There the snow had formed drifts two to three feet high. I made several sudden unscheduled stops. I was feeling my way down the mountain when I suddenly sensed a need to pull up short. Not too soon, it turned out. My skis were overhanging a large cornice. I was looking down at a ten foot vertical drop.

I was congratulating myself on my good fortune when I saw that Joe wasn't going to stop;. Before I could call out, Joe went airborne off the cornice and disappeared into a pile of snow below me.

"Great! I was hoping I wouldn't have to do any patrolling duties today, I said, looking for a way to get to Joe.

But Joe rolled out of a big snow pile and flashed a smile. He was okay. He proceeded to brush off the snow and clear his goggles. "I think it's time for lunch," he said.

We parked our skis in front of the lodge and went upstairs to the lunch room. Sallie and Dottie were already there with the Sunriver crowd. Lunch at Pine Martin Lodge on Wednesdays is filled with much cajoling and riotous conversation among the Sunriverites. After an hour we figured it was time to ski some more or pack it in.

"Let's make one more run," said Sallie.

"Sure, we haven't skied with you at all today. We can make our last run down West Boundary. There is some great powder off to the east side."

"You and your powder, don't you ever get enough?" she asked.

"Not yet, but I suppose someday. Powder skiing is as close to paradise as you can get."

SNOW REMOVAL

By

Frank Allen

A beautiful view greets Rubert every morning in any season, but it is especially pretty when only the trees are visible above the snow. This level of snow has a side effect requiring snow shovels or noisy snow blowers to clear the driveway. Moving to Arizona for the winter is the chicken's way out. Rubert is no chicken. He attacks the snow with the vigor and enthusiasm of a man ten years his junior bending his knees, not his back. Shoveling snow is good exercise and Rubert always has a sense of accomplishment after he finishes. Rubert's big complaint is the huge snowplow that clears the road to make it passable for him and his neighbors.

When there is a six-inch snowfall, the plow moves a cubic yard of snow for every foot of lane length. Rubert's frontage is 30 yards and he has a driveway 20 feet wide. So, the plow driver must shove 30 cubic yards of snow to the side and try not to put any in Rubert's driveway, or Joe's next door, or Pete's across the street. Snow is compacted a little when it is plowed, just like making a snowball but not enough to reduce the volume substantially. No matter how talented the operator, the plow almost always leaves a berm of a few yards of compressed snow in the entrances to driveways.

Rubert thought of a few alternatives to get rid of the snow:

Replace the plows with highway snow blowers and blow the snow into people's yards. No! It could end up in their driveways, on their roofs or breaking windows. The neighbors wouldn't like that.

Use giant heaters and melt the snow. No! Melting would be extremely expensive and cause a disposal problem. Since it is still winter the melted water will flow to the fellow's lot that is on the low side of the road and then freeze, since the ground is still frozen. If we did that, Chuck might get upset.

Compress the snow into billets or blocks with a baler and leave them in the middle of cul-de-sacs or in the commons to melt in the springtime. Kids could make igloos out of them. We could make half size blocks for little kids. Longer lanes would require assistance to carry the cubes to cul de sacs or storage areas. Blocks could be left at the side of the road, but successive snows would leave little space. Toboggan runs could be installed near hilly streets and the cubes slid down hill. Some kids might ride a couple of cubes to the bottom. Snow removal would be entertainment. This solution has promise but also a few problems and will take a little time.

Rubert "Rube" Goldberg decided he would perfect his idea later, but for now, he would just have to put on his jacket and mitts, and get out and shovel the berm.

* * * * * *

SNOW
By
Keith S. Pennington

There were several angry owners on Hoodoo
Who had snow right up the Kazoo
    Driveways six feet deep in white
    Houses totally out of sight.
So they were failed by Design Review!!

WHAT THIS COUNTRY NEEDS
IS
A GOOD $10.00 SNOW SHOVEL

By
Robert C. Antle

And why did you move to Sunriver?

After the initial question, "Where you from?" often the follow up, is "Why?" The answers are as numerous and varied as the birds that frequent Frank Allen's feeder. I have often thought about taking a survey regarding, Why! Just interrogate those newcomers who stand at their first potluck and hesitantly announce, "We're Will and Wilma Wilson from Wasco, Washington". It would be easy to corner the newcomers and get the facts, but being a timid soul, I never did.

But I'll bet shoveling snow would be one of the least likely reasons for a move to Sunriver. Do those super sales people ever ask a prospective buyer, "Do you like winter?" Or a simple question like, "Do you own a shovel?"

My reason for choosing Sunriver was pure and simple-one can ski and golf from one residence. But in all honesty, I was not prepared for the surfeit and the continual peppering of those hexagonal crystals that often become ice. Winters were never kind in Michigan, but living at sea level is vastly different than the high desert at 4200 feet.

When I inspected my old shovel this fall, I found it in sad repair so I scurried to the hardware. The selection was abominable. Fragile red plastic blades with anemic looking handles--much like a child's model, only larger. One had a peculiar looking handle--bend into a S-curve. Like my rafter hung bike, this monstrosity would be another noggin knocker.

"Most men use snow-blowers." With a look of disdain, I replied, "I'm not most men. I'm a traditionalist. I've seen too many butchered hands", I added, and walked out.

Part of my wife's dowry was a beautiful red and black snowblower--used only three times. It was the infamous '93' winter when I announced, "I prefer shoveling, blowers are too dangerous, plus the storage problem". "Oh", was her succinct, surprised reply. Some day I'll tell her the real reason for this distaste for the machine--my limited mechanical ability. Shucks, I even have trouble using a yardstick. Yup, I sold the blower for $150.00. The inundation then began--137 inches clobbered our serene village. An exodus began in the spring, a hegira anywhere to escape winter in Sunriver.

A neighbor, who has his drive plowed, asked, "Buck, how do you keep your drive so free of rutted snow and ice?" "P and P method" was my answer. "What's that?" "Prompt and persistent, it's as simple as that."

Back in 87, when I shared a drive with a nice couple from California, I learned the first 'P'. Get the snow shoveled before they smashed it down with their cars. Otherwise the ruts and ice formed, the bane of every conscientious driveway artisan. The second 'P' comes naturally. Push those lovely flakes off often, sometimes five or six times a day. Promptness and persistence, the ingredients for a shiny blacktop all winter.

Incidentally, a friend, with mechanical ability, repaired my old shovel. I shall continue to use this effective blade, but if it becomes not repairable, or the cloud seeding is successful, I'm out of here.

FIRST SNOW

By
Annis Oetinger

Softly, gently the flakes dress the

Dark branches by my door.

No wind disturbs the white coat

Nor the last leaf clinging to the tree,

Refusing to admit its time is past,

A grace note of red in a black and

White concerto.

HOLIDAY MAGIC

By

Dave Ghormley

If you want to get into the mood for the holidays, I invite you to spend Christmas week at Sunriver. There are loads of holiday parties, families coming and going through the snow, beautiful holiday decorations in everyone's homes, and general *bon vivant* afoot in all directions. You know you are in a magic place when you drive into Sunriver, see all the trees laden down with fresh snow, and the reflection of myriad's of Christmas tree lights reflecting off the snow.

Normally, Sunriver is pretty fussy about outdoor lights. Some of our more politically-correct folks call excess illumination, "light pollution". Whatever the words are for "too many damned bright lights outside", folks get right touchy if their view of the heavens is dimmed or the neighborhood owl has trouble seeing a delicate rodent morsel because of it being under a flood light. It just ain't natural, and a lot of the magic of Sunriver is Nature with a capital N.

However, maybe it's because there are clouds, or maybe its because its so cold outside that no one wants to sit out there and look at the stars anyway. Or maybe its because the only owls out looking for chow are those that got tossed out of the nest by their better halves because they were griping about the cold or the food or something. Whatever it is, folks aren't nearly so fussy about lights at Christmas time. In fact, the whole place goes light-ballistic. It's enough to make the folks at a Chinese light factory swoon with sheer pleasure and disbelief. Now they know where all those stupid lights have been going!

Or maybe its just that we all go nuts over outside

Christmas lights because they really get us into the spirit of the holidays and they just look so doggoned beautiful here in our little tucked-away spot of heaven.

Whatever the reasons, human beings being what they are, there has gradually been more and more competition over who can hang out the most lights, the prettiest displays, the biggest lights, the most creative displays, and so on and so on *ad naseum*. It wouldn't surprise me at all if some formidable lady looking for a new theme for the never ending charity "events" didn't start promoting a serious judging contest for the various classes of light displays. She could be charging visitors $5 to come see our efforts, having bus tours to the winning displays on the first night after the usual $100 per plate fund-raiser, and seeing to it that the local media gives the whole effort suitable publicity.

We're a long ways from such extravaganzas, I guess, but the trend is there. Take what's going on my lane, for example. Three or four years ago a couple of us had some lights along the eaves of our garage. Now, I have a couple of spruce trees out at the edge of our driveway, and my wife has talked me into stringing an extension cord out to them and filling them up with lights. They're beautiful, if I do say so. However, we're peanuts compared to what is going on further down our cul-de-sac. We have some super displays there with lights covering trees, bushes, and twigs. If you walk by at the wrong moment, you might get festooned yourself. The displays have been done with very good taste, and the whole end of the lane is a blaze of beauty and light. Several of the new neighbors have stated that we ain't seen anything yet. Wait till next Christmas and see what they do!

I've pretty much decided to go back to just a few lights on my eaves. I'm not going to compete with what could well be compared to the Crystal Cathedral! One thing I've been thinking about doing is to make a big lighted arrow and point it down the street at the displays at the end. At least this would be a community contribution aimed at keeping the traffic moving and cutting down on the mass confusion of cars full of families trying to figure out how to navigate while "ooh-ing" and "aah-ing" at the lights.

What we have right now is just right. In fact, it's downright beautiful. We thank all who have contributed so much beauty to the community. The place is just downright breathtakingly lovely at holiday time.

We'll let the Board of Directors debate how to find just the right balance between Holiday Magic and mass confusion. That's why we pay them all those big salaries. Ought to keep them occupied for months.